My Life as a Billionaire

Other Books by Janet Tashjian
Illustrated by Jake Tashjian

The My Life Series:
My Life as a Book
My Life as a Stuntboy
My Life as a Cartoonist
My Life as a Joke
My Life as a Gamer
My Life as a Ninja
My Life as a Youtuber
My Life as a Meme
My Life as a Coder

The Einstein the Class Hamster Series:
Einstein the Class Hamster
Einstein the Class Hamster and the Very Real Game Show
Einstein the Class Hamster Saves the Library

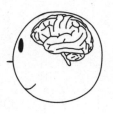

By Janet Tashjian

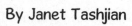

The Marty Frye, Private Eye Series:
Marty Frye, Private Eye: The Case of the Missing Action Figure
Marty Frye, Private Eye: The Case of the Stolen Poodle
Marty Frye, Private Eye: The Case of the Busted Video Games

The Sticker Girl Series:
Sticker Girl
Sticker Girl Rules the School
Sticker Girl and the Cupcake Challenge

The Larry Series:
The Gospel According to Larry
Vote for Larry
Larry and the Meaning of Life

Fault Line
For What It's Worth
Multiple Choice
Tru Confessions

JANET TASHJIAN

My Life as a Billionaire

with cartoons by
JAKE TASHJIAN

Christy Ottaviano Books
Henry Holt and Company
New York

Henry Holt and Company, *Publishers since 1866*
120 Broadway, New York, NY 10271
mackids.com

Henry Holt® is a registered trademark of Macmillan
Publishing Group, LLC
Text copyright © 2021 by Janet Tashjian
Illustrations copyright © 2021 by Jake Tashjian

Our books may be purchased in bulk for promotional,
educational, or business use. Please contact your local
bookseller or the Macmillan Corporate and Premium
Sales Department at (800) 221-7945 ext. 5442 or by
email at MacmillanSpecialMarkets@macmillan.com.

Library of Congress Cataloging-in-Publication Data is
available.

ISBN 978-1-250-26181-6

First Edition, 2021

Printed in the United States of America by LSC
Communications, Harrisonburg, Virginia
10 9 8 7 6 5 4 3 2 1

For Chad

My Life
as a
Billionaire

A CHANCE TO EARN SOME CASH

THE LAST THING I THOUGHT I'D be doing this weekend is carrying mics and amplifiers up three sets of stairs in the sweltering heat. The only person I know who could convince me to sign up for such a lame-o weekend is, of course, Matt.

His brother Jamie's band, Velvet Incinerator, is touring for the next several months and needs help

amplifiers

sweltering

discarded

moving some extra gear into a storage unit. Matt talked me into helping by telling me we could scour the place for cool stuff people discarded and skateboard through the industrial park. But what really got my attention was the forty bucks apiece Jamie said he'd pay us.

I couldn't turn down an opportunity to make some cash doing something outside of chores at home. I had a nice gig doing errands for a few neighbors, but that came to an end when I got carried away playing air guitar and accidently whacked the head off Ms. Clifton's fountain. She immediately took to the neighborhood message thread to share how unhappy she was with my work. My clientele pretty much dried up after that.

The payday from helping Matt's brother will let me afford something I've been itching to buy—a 3D printer. I've saved up for lots of big-ticket items before, mostly having to do with skateboarding. New wheels, new decks, upgraded sneakers— but a 3D printer will be my biggest purchase by far.

My parents have always made a point to try to instill good money sense in me. Their top principle of fiscal responsibility is that saving money is incredibly important. Out of all the different things they've taught me through the years, it's the only one with concrete proof. (See above: wheels, deck, shoes.)

clientele

purchase

instill

fiscal

So when I have the chance to score forty bucks in one day, I take the job to add the cash to my savings.

3D printer, here I come!

GRUNT WORK

"WHAT'S WORSE?" MATT ASKS AS we climb the stairs for the tenth time. "Carrying one big, heavy box or a handful of smaller things?"

"Are the smaller things in one package or are they loose?" I ask.

"Loose."

"Then definitely a bigger box." As evidence, I hold up the reams of paper, old frying pan, and

reams

headphones I'm carrying upstairs. "When Jamie said he and his friends were packed, I thought they'd be ready to go."

Instead, Matt's mom took us to Jamie's apartment this morning and we found him and his friends playing video games on the floor surrounded by moving boxes. EMPTY moving boxes. Matt's mom seemed about as pleased as Matt and I were; she

rustled

rustled the guys to their feet to begin the moving day Jamie had begged us to help him with.

Forty dollars, forty dollars, forty dollars, I tell myself as I dump several loose decks of playing cards into an empty shoebox. I try to focus

tangible

on the fact that I'll have something tangible on the other side of all this work. Matt, on the other hand,

will blow through his allotment by
tomorrow afternoon, probably buying
old comedy albums on eBay.

allotment

By four o'clock, everyone is a
sweaty, dirty mess.

Jamie thrusts his hands into the
front pockets of his jeans and pulls
out the cotton linings. His pockets are
as empty as the moving boxes were.

"I'm going to have to get back
to you with some cash," Jamie tells
us. "Buying all the boxes and tape
wiped me out."

"Those handheld tape dispensers
are EXPENSIVE," his friend Tony
says. "Like four dollars apiece."

dispensers

Before I can protest, Matt beats
me to it.

"You said, 'Be here at ten,' and
we were here at ten. You said, 'Bring
your A game,' and we brought our A

stifles

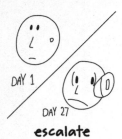

DAY 1 / DAY 27

escalate

game," Matt states firmly. "We did our part, now you do yours."

Jamie looks at his little brother and stifles a laugh. "You'll get your money, Mattster, just not today."

I know Matt hates it when Jamie calls him "Mattster" and hope Jamie didn't just escalate an already-prickly situation.

Matt turns to his mom, who looks at both her sons and shrugs. Matt's mom is much more hands-off than mine. Most of the time I think that's a good thing, but today I want her to stick up for Matt and lay down the law.

As Matt and Jamie argue, I do some mental math and figure my 3D printer got pushed back at least another month.

"Okay, okay, okay," Jamie tells

Matt. "Just so I don't have to listen to you anymore." He rummages around for his jacket and pulls out a Powerball ticket.

"THAT COST YOU TWO BUCKS, not forty!" Matt shouts. "Besides, we want money—not a stupid lottery ticket."

He shifts his attention from Matt to me. "How about you, Derek? You feeling lucky?"

"No, Jamie," I answer. "I'm looking for real money too."

"This thing could be worth millions!" Jamie continues.

"The odds are a zillion to one that it's worth nothing," Matt argues.

Tony lets out a low whistle while scrolling through his phone. "The payout's over a billion dollars right now. You could be RICH."

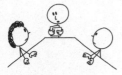

arbitration

Matt turns to his mother for arbitration one more time but she shakes her head and leaves the room. For Matt's mom, not getting involved with a sibling squabble is nonnegotiable.

As upset as I am about Jamie's lame offer, the prospect of owning a lottery ticket is tempting.

"Are we even allowed to HAVE lottery tickets?" I ask. "I didn't think it was legal for kids to gamble."

"It's not gambling," Jamie said. "It's a harmless game of chance."

stiff

"That's what gambling IS!" Matt shouts. "Not only did you stiff us on the pay, now you're trying to get us in trouble too?"

I snatch the lottery ticket from Jamie's hand. "You can pay me with this, but you still owe Matt."

Anything to move this day along and get home. Dinner, my dog, Bodi, video games—I have a dozen more interesting things to do tonight than this.

"Deal." Jamie slaps my back and Matt and I head to the car.

At this rate, I'll get my 3D printer just in time to print myself some dentures.

dentures

IT'S IMPOSSIBLE

nationwide

nil

BACK HOME THAT NIGHT, I DON'T bother showing my parents the lottery ticket. I'm usually pretty optimistic but even I realize the chances of winning a nationwide lottery are pretty much nil. Besides, I know what Mom would focus on—that you have to be eighteen to buy a lottery ticket, so I shouldn't even have one; that I couldn't claim the jackpot even if I won; that Jamie should respect Matt's and my time; and so on. Since I can predict everything she'll say, there's no reason to broach the subject; I remove the ticket from my back pocket where the forty dollars should've been and toss it on my desk.

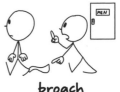

broach

My parents have already eaten and are playing Boggle in the living room. Mom tells me to help myself to some baked ziti, then join them for a family tournament.

tournament

Both my parents have been on a campaign to reduce time spent with technology—which is maybe the worst idea they've ever had. So instead of scrolling through TikTok, Instagram, or YouTube after school and on weekends, I end up playing a lot of board games or reading. I have a reading disability, so books aren't my first choice, although drawing pictures of my vocabulary words in my notebook is something I've come to enjoy. I'm hoping this "old-fashioned fun" idea of theirs will eventually fall by the wayside the way composting and making our own soap did.

Bodi's curled underneath the coffee table beside my usual place on the couch. My parents have the TV on the news station in the background, yet ANOTHER great idea of theirs about how everyone needs to stay well-versed in current events. After the evacuation and wildfires last year, Dad has become a news junkie. I liked it better when we watched Westerns or comedies

well-versed

for the third and fourth time instead of watching all this NEWS.

Even though reading isn't my best subject, Boggle is actually one of my favorite games. Sure, they're both focused on words, but at least with Boggle you get to shake all the cubes in the little container first. Maybe if books were more tactile, I'd have better luck with them.

tactile

When we tally the scores from the first round, I'm disappointed that the longest word I found—*DEEPEN*—doesn't count because I used the same *E* twice. To me, it's a technicality, but Mom's a stickler for following rules, so I end up not getting credit for it.

technicality

When the woman comes on the last segment of the local news to

stickler

read the Powerball numbers, I don't bother looking up. But as I'm staring at the cubes to find new words, I hear her say "27," which I remember was the first number on Jamie's ticket. When she picks up the second Ping-Pong ball and reads the number "15," I sit up straight in my chair. Even if the first two numbers are the same as the ones Jamie chose, it's still a zillion to one the others will match. I excuse myself from Boggle and run upstairs to find the Powerball ticket on my desk.

By the time I flatten the paper and hurry downstairs, there are now three Ping-Pong balls sitting on the little shelf beside the woman. 27 15 59. I stare at the paper in my hand listing the same three numbers.

"Your turn to tally up," Dad says.

"Although neither of us will be able to catch up to your mom after that last round. How did she find the word *straighten*?"

Mom doesn't miss a beat and asks what's in my hand. I tell her Jamie gave me his lottery ticket today.

"You have to be eighteen..."

"I know!" I snap. "But these first three numbers match."

Dad grimaces as if that couldn't possibly be true but is intrigued enough to read the ticket over my shoulder.

grimaces

"44," the woman on TV says.

My dad and I look from the ticket stub to each other. The next number on the paper in my hand is ALSO 44.

Mom jumps up and joins us. "That's incredible! What are the chances the next one is..."

"63," the woman says.

All three of us scream. Bodi jumps to his feet and starts barking his head off. I rub his neck to get him to relax, but he can tell something exciting is going on.

"Okay, calm down," Dad says. "This is a giant fluke—there's absolutely no way the last number is..."

"8!" the woman announces.

My hands are shaking as I stare at the ticket in my hand. An 8.

I trace my fingers along the row of numbers and match them to the Ping-Pong balls on-screen. 27 15 59 44 63 8. This time we're all too shocked to scream.

"Well, that's tonight's Powerball number—good luck to all our viewers," the woman says. "Remember the jackpot tonight is one point six BILLION dollars."

My mother shakes her head. "Did she say million with an M?" She looks at us both cautiously. "Or billion with a B?"

"Billion with a B," my father and I answer.

My mom slowly lowers herself onto the couch. I'm guessing she's got a million—with an M—questions, but right now the gears in her brain are completely clogged by the near impossibility of what just happened.

clogged

I grab Bodi's paws and dance.

I AM NOW A BILLIONAIRE!!!

I SPOKE TOO SOON

THE NEXT HOUR IS SPENT ON MY dad's laptop examining the rules and regulations for Powerball in the state of California. Mom's right—you do have to be eighteen to purchase a lottery ticket, which means I won't be able to claim the winnings myself. Another fact is that you have up to a year to bring in a winning ticket, which

inevitable

leads to the inevitable question—

WHAT KIND OF KNUCKLEHEAD WAITS A YEAR TO PICK UP THAT MUCH MONEY?

While my parents make notes on the proper procedures, I focus on

procedures

something else—Jamie. Of course, I can't wait to tell Matt, Carly, and Umberto about this incredible bonanza, but I'm worried about

bonanza

Jamie's reaction. Will he be happy that someone he knows actually won or will he try to get me to give him back the ticket? I put myself in his shoes and think about what I'd do if the situation were reversed. I hate

reversed

to admit it, but I'd use every possible argument to get that winning ticket back. So when my parents and I finally get ready for bed, I tell them I want to go to the lottery office tomorrow, BEFORE I tell Matt and

Jamie. As usual, Mom sees through my ploy immediately.

"First of all," she begins, "the lottery office isn't open on a Sunday."

"Can't we just go to a place that sells lottery tickets to cash it in?"

Dad shakes his head. "Not for that much money. I don't know any 7-Elevens with a billion dollars on hand."

Mom sits on the edge of my bed. "I think it's important to have an open conversation with Jamie about this, don't you?"

"He's going to say he bought the ticket and the money is his!"

"Then I think you have to work through that with him," Mom continues. "You've been friends with Matt and his family for years—you don't

want something like this coming between you."

"I'd rather split the money with
Matt than Jamie," I say.

Dad shakes his head and laughs.
"I actually feel bad for Jamie—
that'll be the last time he tries to
hoodwink someone out of an honest
day's pay."

hoodwink

"Come on," I plead. "We can go to
the lottery office first thing Monday
morning—I can hold off telling Matt
till then."

"No way," Mom says. "We're
doing this aboveboard and by the
book the whole way."

"Don't forget, Monday is a school
day," Dad adds.

"You CAN'T expect me to go to
school when there's a billion dollars
on the line!"

Mom stands and makes her way into the hall. "If this money is already starting to have a negative effect, you may be better off without it."

"That's not even remotely possible," I answer.

I barely sleep after the light goes off, partly from the excitement but mostly because I'm worried Jamie's going to try to sabotage this the second he finds out.

TO TELL OR NOT
TO TELL

BEFORE I EVEN OPEN MY EYES THE next morning, the magnitude of my new situation causes me to bolt out of bed. I have to compile a list of stuff to buy immediately! For months I've been thinking nonstop about that 3D printer, but that seems like small potatoes compared to what $1.6 billion can buy. I can

magnitude

nonstop

probably afford to purchase a 3D printer COMPANY now.

I tear into my backpack for a notebook and flip to a fresh page. My hand can't keep up with all the things I can afford with my winnings. Backyard skateboard park, new bike, go-cart, giant screen TV, video games—the list is endless. Besides the stuff for myself, I brainstorm the ocean of presents I can get for my parents and friends too.

Mom's always mentioning how nice a home gym would be and Dad's told me countless times how much he wishes he'd learned to play the banjo from his grandpa. Personally, I think my parents would also look pretty cool in a new Tesla. I can treat Carly to a shopping spree, and maybe buy Umberto a new wheelchair. Matt and I can get all the designer skate gear we want, or spend a day with one of our favorite comedians on a fundraiser auction site. The sky's the limit with this much cash!

Bodi enters my room and curls up on the carpet. "I wonder if they make a rocket-powered skateboard for dogs," I ask him. "Or an extreme obstacle course!" I pivot to my laptop to do a search, but the sound of Bodi's heavy breathing makes me reconsider. He's not exactly the boisterous, energetic pup he used to be. These days he can barely hop up on my bed.

boisterous

I scoot back in my chair and bring my laptop down to join him on the carpet. "Let's find you something nice and relaxing. How does that sound? Gourmet meals? A personal masseuse for world-class belly rubs?" I type *luxury dog relaxation* into the search bar and up pops a wide array of high-end dog beds. "Hey, this one's real mink." I enlarge the picture to show him. "That HAS to be classy."

The only thing that stops me from spending an entire day adding to my shopping list is a text from Matt. He wants to go skateboarding to make up for the grueling day of helping his brother yesterday. He doesn't mention anything about the lottery ticket, so when I text him back, I don't either.

grueling

As soon as Matt steps into the kitchen, he knows something's up by the look on my face.

"Okay, spill it," he says. "Your

dad's working on a new movie and we get to go on set?"

It's uncanny how well Matt knows me; I OBVIOUSLY can't hide my windfall forever, so I make him guess.

uncanny

"Allowance increase? Bodi's got a girlfriend? YOU'VE got a girl-friend?" He laughs at his own joke. "Considering I was with you all day yesterday, it would be pretty difficult to have started a relationship this morning."

allowance

"I'll give you a hint—it DOES have something to do with yesterday."

"You're going to take Tony's advice and get a set of drums?"

Just as I'm beginning to think having Matt guess is a bad idea, his expression turns to shock.

"NOT THE LOTTERY TICKET?"

I nod.

"What'd you hit? Fifty bucks? A hundred? Let's go to the comic book store!"

I point to the ceiling, gesturing up.

"A thousand? Ten thousand?!"

Matt runs around the kitchen like the Energizer Bunny. "Are you going to tell me you won a million dollars?"

"Uhmm...one point six billion." Before he can ask me to clarify I add, "Billion with a B."

Matt grabs me and lifts me into the air. I hadn't really noticed how he's gotten so much stronger lately. "A BILLION DOLLARS?"

"One point six. Although they take taxes out. I don't know all the details." As excited as I am to share this news with my best friend, part of me is waiting for the other shoe to drop—then it does.

"You mean JAMIE could've been a billionaire?" Matt shakes his head. "He's going to go NUTS!"

I don't tell Matt that I've been thinking the same thing.

Matt sits down at the kitchen table. "I mean, technically, HE'S the one who selected those specific numbers..."

selected

I lower myself onto the chair beside him. "Yeah, but he GAVE me the ticket. It was his choice to pay me that way, not mine."

I can almost see the wheels turn in Matt's brain—how different things would be if Jamie had had forty bucks in his pocket yesterday instead of a winning lottery ticket.

"I mean, you two COULD split it," Matt suggests. "That's certainly enough money to go around."

"There wasn't enough money to go around yesterday when it was time to pay me for a day's work." I don't like the direction this conversation is taking and bet Matt and I won't be skateboarding after this.

Sure enough, Matt tells me he's heading home. "I want to tell Jamie before he hears it on the news or something."

"I was GOING to tell him," I stammer. "I just found out last night!"

scenarios

Matt nods, but I can tell he's running different scenarios through his head.

"Dude, we'll be able to upgrade all our gear!" I say. "Think of all the cool stuff we can do."

"Absolutely." Matt smiles as he goes outside.

I know he's happy for me but I also know he's thinking that money could've belonged to HIS family, not mine.

Less than twenty minutes later, Jamie shows up at the back door and shoves two twenty-dollar bills into my hand.

"This is for yesterday," he says. "I really appreciate your help."

I hand him back the money and tell him he already paid me.

Jamie rubs the back of his neck. "Yeah, about that . . . I've been playing those same Powerball numbers for almost a year. I kind of feel like I'M the one who made this happen, not you."

"No one made this happen!" I shake my head. "It's one hundred percent chance. The odds were a trillion to one."

paces

Jamie still can't look me in the eyes as he paces around the kitchen. "You have to be eighteen to claim it," he says. "So you need me for that part anyway."

"My parents can claim it. We read up on all the rules last night." I'm thinking this could get ugly fast and am relieved when Mom comes downstairs and asks if we're okay.

"How could I POSSIBLY be okay?" Jamie says. "I stupidly gave Derek my winning lottery ticket!"

"Maybe the stupid part was not

planning ahead to pay someone who busted their butt to help you," I say. The fact that I'M giving someone grief for not planning ahead seems ridiculous, even to me.

"I'm sure you two can talk this through," Mom says. "And if you can't work it out, I'd be happy to claim the money myself and donate every penny to charity. It could certainly do real good combating hunger around the world."

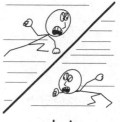

combating

This shuts up both Jamie and me immediately. Leave it to Mom to get to the bottom of things FAST.

When she leaves the room, Jamie looks at me directly for the first time since he's been here. "Dude! I'm going on tour. The band has momentum. I can use that money!"

momentum

"Join the club." I don't mention

the 3D printer I've been dreaming about for months.

"Should we split it?" Jamie asks. "Is that fair?"

I spent hours last night in bed pondering this exact question.

possession

On the one hand, I had NOTHING to do with choosing those winning numbers. On the other hand, if possession is nine-tenths of the law—something they always say on cop shows—then the ticket is mine. To be honest, the money is a gift, a surprise from the universe. I don't even know if it's possible to spend a billion and a half dollars in a lifetime.

"If we DID split it," I ask, "will Matt get some? You wouldn't just keep it all for yourself?"

"The whole family will benefit," Jamie answers. "With that much money I can buy my parents a new house."

"But you probably won't, right?" I know Jamie well enough to know he'd buy himself a house before he bought one for Matt and his parents.

I also realize once we split it— IF we split it—the last thing I want to do is start to monitor Jamie's spending.

monitor

"27, 15, 59, 44, 63, 8," Jamie says. "Those numbers have MEANING for me. 27 in honor of the club the greatest rock stars belong to. I was 15 when I got my first kiss. '59 for the year of my grandfather's Corvette. The first election I got to vote in was for the 44th president. 63 was the score I got on my calculus final—I passed the class and was able to graduate! And 8 was how old I was when I first picked up a guitar. Those numbers came from my life and they hit! Come on, Derek, you know I'm right."

This is one of those times I wish my parents WOULD tell me what to do. The stakes couldn't be higher. But they are die-hard believers that all decisions from small to gigantic should be teaching moments. We decided they'd help me manage the winnings either way, but what I decide to do about Jamie is MY decision. With this much money on the table, they STILL refuse to interfere. But even without their input, I know what I want to do.

I extend my hand to Jamie and tell him we'll split the winnings fifty-fifty. He pulls me in for a hug and

die-hard

refuse

interfere

lifts me off the ground the same way Matt did earlier.

"Let's claim it first thing Monday morning!" Jamie says.

"Uhm...my parents are making me go to school."

I can see Jamie's about to make the same argument I made—that collecting a billion dollars is WAY more important than algebra or history—but he doesn't want to push his luck.

$$a \times (b \times c)$$
$$(a \times b) + (a \times c)$$

algebra

"After school Monday it is."

When he leaves, my parents suddenly appear; I'm sure they were listening to every word from the living room.

"Was it worth eight hundred million dollars to let me come to that decision on my own?" I ask them.

unequivocally

Dad doesn't seem as sure as Mom, who answers immediately, "Unequivocally yes."

And just like that I go from billionaire with a B to millionaire with an M.

A NICE REACTION

UMBERTO IS AT HIS AUNT'S HOUSE when I call with the news; he's so excited, he makes me tell every single one of his relatives before he'll hang up. Carly is downright jubilant when I text her and breaks the land-speed record running over to my house.

jubilant

"OMG OMG OMG, this is incredible!"

Before I can stop her—not that I would—Carly jumps into my arms and gives me a giant hug. I tell her about the ticket and splitting the money with Jamie.

"Who cares if you have to split it?" she says. "It's still more money than you've ever dreamed of, right?"

If I was feeling even a tiny bit of remorse about partnering with Jamie, Carly's positive attitude gets me back on track.

partnering

"I'm sure you've already thought about all the great nonprofits you can give your money to."

I don't tell her that I actually haven't given that any thought at all.

contribution

"You should think about making a contribution to the Greta Thunberg Foundation. They're doing great things in terms of sustainability."

"Leave it to you to talk about giving my money away before I even

sustainability

HAVE it!" I give her a good-natured nudge. "Between you and my mom, I'll definitely be giving money to charity, so I want to hear your ideas."

As much as Carly champions several causes, she's been following Greta Thunberg's work and talks about her pretty much nonstop. It IS kind of amazing how a teenager from Sweden has become the international face for climate change. I'm not as kooky as Carly is when it comes to the subject, but Greta's determination and passion are definitely impressive.

"Okay, let's see your list," Carly says. "Besides the 3D printer."

I run upstairs and grab my notebook with the list of future purchases. Before I head back to show her, I rip out the page with the stuff I want to get family and friends; I may not have decided on charitable donations yet, but I've certainly thought about fun gifts for Carly, Matt, Umberto, and my parents.

This year, it's Christmas 24/7!

BMOC

WHEN I GET TO SCHOOL MONDAY morning, Matt has already told EVERY SINGLE PERSON that Jamie and I won the lottery. The way he tells the story, he's an integral part of the process. "If I hadn't dragged Derek with me to help my brother—who's now ALSO a zillionaire—none of this would've happened. All this cash and I'M the catalyst!"

integral

catalyst

reclaim

Matt is so excited that I let him run with the story. (Normally I'd try to reclaim some of the glory, but did I mention I'm cashing in a winning lottery ticket after school?)

Ms. McCoddle does a little dance when I enter the classroom, which makes me think she might be spending a lot of time on TikTok. She grabs my arm and twirls me around, then leads me to my desk. The first twenty minutes of class are spent talking about how lucky I am; after that, she goes around the room asking each of us what we'd do with that much money.

Dylan suggests buying a sports team; Timothy says even a billion dollars couldn't buy the Lakers or Clippers, but maybe the Kings. Natalie immediately brings up the

Greta Thunberg Foundation, which makes me wonder if everyone on the planet is now obsessed with this young Swedish activist. Umberto makes a pitch for setting up a media wing in our school with computers, drawing tablets, 3D printers, green screens, and all the latest designing and editing software. It's a fabulous idea that I mentally put on my list.

"Actually, lotteries were held even before the thirteen colonies won their independence," Ms. McCoddle says. "In fact, the Continental Congress held a ten-million-dollar lottery to help finance the Revolutionary War."

Continental

"I'd love to do the math and see what that's worth in today's dollars," Umberto says.

myriad

scamming

speculation

Only Umberto would perform a calculation like that for fun.

Ms. McCoddle suddenly gets serious, warning me about not falling for the myriad of people who make their living scamming—not only IRL but on the Internet. She's 100 percent right, of course, it's just a downer after all that speculation about all the fun stuff I can do with that much money.

Most of the school day is a blur, with kids I barely know congratulating me in the halls. I keep checking the time to see how much longer before Jamie, my parents, and I head to Chatsworth—a town I've never heard of—to the California lottery office. By the time the end-of-the-day bell finally rings, I'm out the doors before most of my classmates even reach their lockers. Matt jumps into Jamie's old convertible and I hop into Dad's SUV. It's time to cash in this ticket!

convertible

MAKING IT OFFICIAL

hightail

uncharted

I ASK DAD TO HIGHTAIL IT TO THE Valley but he's doing his best to make sure we all stay calm. "This is uncharted territory for all of us," he says. "We need to take things one step at a time."

I try to take him seriously, but it's difficult when Matt is in the next lane on the 405 hanging out of

Jamie's car, screaming and yelling to get my attention.

When Dad grabs a spot in the parking lot thirty minutes later, Matt, Jamie, and I make a beeline for the receptionist desk. He points us to the office where we need to go and fill out the paperwork to claim our winnings.

beeline

receptionist

When Mom catches up, she gives Matt and Jamie a big smile, but I can see she's having a difficult time with this. Even though winning the lottery is good news—make that GREAT news—Mom's doing what she always does and looking ten steps ahead. I've watched enough animal documentaries to know it's something most mothers in the animal kingdom do, but I wish she'd just let herself be excited for once without worrying about the future—and hopefully imaginary—problems.

unruffled

Since Jamie is the one who bought the ticket, he approaches the woman at the desk. I would've thought she'd seen enough lottery winners to be pretty unruffled by the whole thing, but she jumps up from her seat and throws handfuls of confetti at Jamie. It turns out she's only been working at the lottery office for a few weeks and he's her first big winner.

Jamie fills out the paperwork—they especially want to know where he bought the ticket—and several people who also work in the office come over to congratulate him. I didn't realize more than one person could win a Powerball at the same time, but three other people in the country ALSO picked that same string of numbers, which means the total pot has to be divided between them too. I try not to think about how my slice of the pie has continually gotten smaller and smaller since they announced the winning number. Instead, I adopt Carly's point of view and am happy with the fact that I have any of the pie at all.

continually

I'm okay in math, but the numbers and percentages getting thrown around are WAY over my head, maybe even over Umberto's. The good news is California doesn't collect state tax on lottery winnings. The bad news is that the federal government takes out a whopping 24 percent before you even get the money. The big discussion is whether Jamie and I will take our (his) winnings up front or spread out the total over the next thirty years.

vetoed

Jamie and I immediately suggest one lump sum but are vetoed by both sets of parents, who insist that spreading the money out over three decades would be better for both of us in the long run. But what wins Jamie and me over to their side of the argument is that you get LESS money if you take it all at once. Decision done.

The director of the lottery commission comes out to talk to Jamie and take some photos. I'm about to jump in front of the camera too when I feel Mom tugging the back of my shirt.

"Jamie is the official winner," she reminds me yet again.

"I know," I tell her for the millionth time. As much as I hate to admit it, I guess I AM having a hard time watching Jamie getting showered with all this attention.

"Your name is now public record. You might get lots of unwanted phone calls and emails." When the director smiles for the camera, I can see his teeth are capped. "The retailer who sold you the winning ticket will be getting lots of attention too."

unwanted

retailer

Matt, Jamie, and I smile at the thought of Jerry, who runs our local 7-Eleven, making the most of this free publicity. Knowing Jerry, he's already hanging signs and banners up and down Westwood Boulevard.

After Jamie finally finishes signing all the paperwork, we leave the office calmly, then go completely bananas in the parking lot. Once we're back at my house, Jamie and I sign a contract that both families' lawyers drew up today. My parents sign alongside me since I'm underage.

"NOW do we get the money?" I ask.

"The director said we'll get the first installment in six to eight weeks," Jamie said.

"That's almost two months!" I whine. "I was going to go pick up my new printer today."

My dad laughs. "I think we can front you the money."

Let the spending begin!

installment

EVERYBODY'S GOT A HAND OUT

JAMIE AND I HAVEN'T RECEIVED the first installment yet—I'll be at his house the second he does, believe me—but that doesn't stop almost every person who's ever met me from dropping hints about stuff they need.

Natalie tells me how her smartphone fell in the toilet and she can't afford a new one, Peter

bawling

mentions how great his YouTube channel would be if he could only buy more viewers, and Abby spends ten minutes in the lunch line bawling about the two rescue dogs she'd love to adopt but can't afford the vaccinations for. When Dad complains about how old his bike is, I can't decide if he's just making conversation or hoping I'll be the one to buy him a new one.

I've been putting some thought into what kind of charities I want to donate to and sprint over to Mom's office with a new idea.

"I want to make a donation to Helping Hands," I tell her as she slips off her latex gloves. "Not just for Frank, but for ALL the capuchins."

Helping Hands is an organization

I've had a lot of experience with. They train capuchins to be service companions for people with special needs. I was lucky enough to foster one of their best companions-in-training of all time—an adorable capuchin named Frank—until I broke the rules and put his safety at risk staging tricks for him to perform on my YouTube channel. As much as I miss Frank, I know he's making a huge difference in some other lucky person's life.

staging

The way Mom smiles at my suggestion makes me wonder if she already thought of this but was waiting to see if I'd come up with the idea on my own.

"They'd really be able to expand," Mom says. "I think they'd be thrilled."

corgi

examination

One of the vet techs brings in Mom's next patient, a corgi with a plastic cone around her neck.

"Maybe we can make the donation in person and spend some time with Frank," Mom suggests. "Visit Grammy at the same time."

"I can buy the airline tickets!" I say.

Mom tousles my hair before heading into the examination room. "You're still our kid," Mom says. "Just because you have money now doesn't mean you have to pay for everything."

Good, I think as I make my way back to the house, *because it looks like I'll be buying smartphones, subscribers, and pet vaccinations soon*. As I open the front door, I make a decision: If I'm going to have money, being generous is my new thing.

Right after I get my 3D printer.

That afternoon when Dad drives me to the mall, I can hardly wait for him to turn the car off before I throw open the door and race to the electronics store. They offered to ship my new 3D printer to our house, but I insisted on picking it up in person so I can start using it ASAP.

At the counter, I'm greeted by a woman with a headset and tablet. "You must be Derek." She smiles.

When I tell her I am, she presses the mic on her headset and asks the person on the other end to bring out the printer my dad prepaid for online.

Another associate wheels over

a dolly with the box containing my 3D printer balanced on the end. When he carefully places it onto the counter, I immediately try to pick it up.

"I wouldn't do that," he says. "This baby weighs eighty-five pounds. You'll need some help getting it out to the parking lot."

"My dad and I can probably handle it." I don't take my hands off the box.

dolly

Dad signs the pickup receipt and tells the associate we could definitely use the help. I ask the guy if I can pull the dolly too and am psyched when he agrees. I feel like a king strolling through the parking garage and can't believe I'm finally going to be able to make some action figures in the comfort of my own room.

Once we're home, I waste no time tearing the box open and setting the printer up. I unwrap the spool of plastic filament, which looks a lot like fishing wire, and clamp it to the top rod. Then I feed the filament down to the heating nozzle. I've watched so many tutorials online that I barely need to consult the instruction manual. Plus, I begged my parents to spring for the preassembled model, so that cuts down on connecting the robotic attachments.

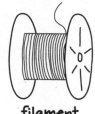

filament

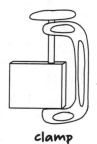

clamp

I plug the printer in and install the design studio software on my laptop while it warms up. Even watching the machine calibrate is amazing. The sound of the tiny robot motor whirring as it zips vertically and horizontally is so cool, I consider making it my ringtone.

calibrate

I've been sketching out potential model designs for weeks—I'm particularly proud of the wheel and axle setup to turn my phone into a toy car—but decide on something simple for the initial test run: one of my signature stick figure drawings with the word *BILLIONAIRE* underneath it. I load the file to the SD card and practically have goose bumps as I insert it into the printer's drive.

"Hold on, hold on!" Mom bursts in from the kitchen drying her hands on a dish towel. "I want to get this on film!"

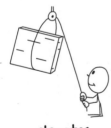

elevates

She pulls out her phone just as the build plate elevates and the hot end slides into position. Both Dad and I hold our breath waiting for the first layer of plastic to form.

"IT'S HAPPENING!" I shout.

I'm typically not a patient person, but my eyes are glued to the nozzle as it darts back and forth, bringing my stick figure to life.

Less than two hours later, I'm proudly holding my very first 3D-printed creation.

I can get used to being rich.

BITTEN BY THE BUG

I DON'T HAVE TO BUG JAMIE TO fork over my half of the money when it finally comes; he and Matt appear at my house with the check from the state and another one made out to me for half that amount.

Even though it's almost nine o'clock on a school night, my parents drive me to the ATM so I can deposit the check immediately. Last week, we opened a joint bank account so my parents will also have to sign if I want to write any checks. But I DID talk them into letting me use the credit card—with permission—that comes with the savings account. I'd be lying if I said I didn't feel TOTALLY cool tucking that baby into a slot in my Velcro wallet.

joint

It takes two days for the check to clear, but when it does, I can't wait to get cracking on my list.

Velcro

"Wait one minute." Mom closes my laptop as soon as I open it. "Let's go over the guidelines."

"AGAIN?"

Instead of answering, she crosses her arms in front of her. When I turn to Dad, he just shrugs.

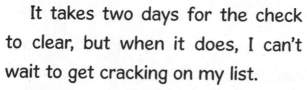

guidelines

I sigh and count down on my fingers what we've been discussing for

stockpiling

annuity

weeks. "We're stockpiling a chunk for college right off the bat. I've got an annuity for the next thirty years. One of you has to approve all purchases over a hundred dollars." I probably would feel stifled by all these rules if I wasn't focused on the fact that I FINALLY have access to my money.

"I think Derek understands the importance of being financially responsible," Dad says.

Mom gives me her blessing by opening my laptop, then heading next door to her office.

"Don't make me regret this," Dad tells me. "I know you've got a lot of money now, but you're still our kid and need to follow the rules."

I tell him okay and thank him for believing in me, but responsibility is the last thing on my mind right now.

Here's what I buy in the first hour of my freedom—WITH my parents' permission:

- Six pairs of high-end designer headphones, one in every color
- Ten shatterproof phone cases
- Eleven battery chargers
- Three new skateboards
- Two pairs of Vans, three pairs of high-tops
- 365 days' worth of candy
- Every game they sell for the Sony PlayStation
- A COMPLETE set of vintage Pokémon cards, including the original holographic foil Charizard

holographic

I also pay for services too, most notably a thirty-minute FaceTime call with Tony Hawk where Matt and I spend more time jumping around the room with excitement than getting tips from him.

"Okay," Matt says. "We can rent the entire Magic Mountain theme park for a hundred thousand dollars an hour."

I can't tell what's more disturbing—such a ridiculously high amount or the fact that Matt just said *we*. I tell him that sounds like a lot of money.

"It's a drop in the bucket for you!" He suddenly snaps his fingers with a new idea. "You should get a robot!" He shakes his head. "No, a driver! Someone to chauffeur us around so our parents don't have to."

chauffeur

His creativity is contagious. "No, a butler," I say. "Like Alfred in *Batman*!"

Matt disagrees. "A bodyguard!"

"With an arsenal of weapons?" I ask.

arsenal

"Yes! And a tank!"

"I was kidding!" I tell Matt we should move away from the impractical purchases and steer the conversation back to reality.

"A BMX bike?" he suggests.

"A BMX wheelchair," I reply. "So Umberto can skate with us."

We both immediately stop pacing the room and stare at each other.

"That's a GREAT idea," Matt says. "I saw this guy on YouTube at the Venice skate park in his chair—he was insane!"

"See? I DO have good ideas... sometimes."

"I've got a good idea." Matt rubs his stomach. "Let's order a pizza, have it delivered, and keep brainstorming cool things to buy."

I tell Matt he's got himself a deal. How can anyone brainstorm without brainfood?

A NEW FULL-TIME JOB

I APPROACH UMBERTO OUTSIDE his locker before first period. "Okay," I begin. "There's something I've been thinking about and want to see if you're up for it."

"If you want to give me a huge chunk of money because I'm the coolest kid you know, I'll have to stop you there." Umberto doesn't even try to keep a straight face.

bestowing

"I'm loaded down with cash as it is," he continues, "so if you're thinking of bestowing me with a million dollars, let me save you some time." He slams his locker shut and spins around to face me with a devilish grin.

"Gee, that's too bad because I've been looking at all these cool new wheelchairs online." I show him the photo on my phone of the most extreme wheelchair on the planet. "It's called the—"

"The full-suspension WCMX chair!" Umberto finishes my sentence with the biggest smile I've ever seen. "I've been watching videos of guys shredding the pavement in these things for years."

"So you know it's got a unique floating rear axle for popping side

unique

wheelies, skateboard wheels on the frog legs, and Kevlar upholstery—that's the stuff they use to make bulletproof vests!" I swipe through the order specifications. "Everything about this bad boy is completely tailor-made to fit your measurements. It'll fit like a glove AND you'll be able to zoom down ramps at lightning speed."

When Umberto looks up at me, his eyes are full of gratitude and maybe a few tears. "I don't know what to say. All I've ever wanted is to join you and Matt at the skate park. That chair can open up a whole WORLD of possibilities!"

But he shakes his head when he sees the price. "No way, dude, that's too much money."

"Not for me." As soon as the

sentence leaves my mouth, I feel like an idiot. "I mean, it would make me very happy to get this for you. Consider it an early birthday present."

"Are you sure?" Umberto asks. "REALLY sure?"

"One hundred percent positively sure," I answer.

Umberto wheels down the hall urging me to keep up. "I've got to call my mom. She'll never believe it!"

I can't wipe the smile off my face for the rest of the day. I remember once in second grade when it was my birthday and Mom brought in two trays of cupcakes so we could have a party in Ms. Talbot's class. It made me so happy to dole out those cupcakes and goodie bags to my classmates that I still remember the

dole

feeling. It's funny how that moment years ago pops into my head as I hand Carly her present today.

Inside is the pair of wireless earbuds she's been looking at since losing her regular ones on the plane when she visited her cousins in Seattle. She tilts her head to the side the way she always does when she's taken aback. "Derek, you didn't have to get me these."

aback

I point to the bag still in her hand. "The rest of your present is inside."

She pulls out the check I'd tucked inside the gift bag made out to the Greta Thunberg Foundation. "No, no." She backs away from me. "This check has way too many zeroes."

"You should be the one to send it to her," I say. "The foundation is only getting that money because of you."

Carly looks about to cry. "You are such a good person, Derek Fallon."

"I know."

Carly crying and the look of thanks she gives me makes me want to contribute every single dollar to make the world a better place.

Almost.

SPENDING SPREE!

MY PARENTS HAVEN'T STOPPED talking about financial advisers and wise investing, but the only thing I want to do when the weekend comes around is buy stuff.

advisers

It felt great to order Umberto's wheelchair and donate to Carly's favorite cause, but now it's time to get some more things for ME.

investing

I'm never one to spend time

in stores or malls, but I can't wait to get some cool new sneakers. Matt's been dying to check out the new store on Melrose that has a line around the block every time we drive by. As much as waiting in line is something I usually avoid at all costs, it feels cool to wait in line here; we even ask Dad to drop us off a block away so we can seem a bit more independent.

cosign

"Now remember what we talked about," Dad tells me. "You can use the new credit card to buy two pairs at the most. Any more than that and I'll have to cosign. Besides, you already have a giant pile of sneakers in your room."

"I know, I know." Mom's words echo in my head too. *You can only wear one pair of shoes at a time.*

Matt and I have always loved people-watching, and the line of people waiting to check out new and vintage designer kicks does not disappoint. Skateboarders, rappers, even an actor from an old Nickelodeon show, who posts updates from his phone while he waits. When we finally make it to the giant double doors, I'm shocked at the rows and rows of boxes lined up to the ceiling.

rappers

Matt zooms across the store to a neon-lit display case filled with the fanciest sneakers I've ever seen. "We're gonna be kings of the skate park in shoes like these."

"We?" I ask.

"Well, yeah," Matt says. "Your dad said you could break in that new credit card with two pairs—one for you, one for me, right? He gave you permission."

Before I can tell Matt that's not exactly what I had in mind, he yanks me by the arm to the other end of the display.

"Whoa!" Matt says. "They have a pair of Red October Yeezys!" He presses his face against the glass case.

aficionado

"You must be a real aficionado." A clerk with turquoise hair and a nose ring walks over. She, Matt, and I discuss the infamous sneaker that Kanye created for Nike before he partnered with Adidas.

infamous

"I'm totally getting these," Matt says. "I take a size ten."

"Unfortunately this is the only pair we have," the clerk frowns. "And they're a nine."

"What a coincidence, my size exactly." I mostly say it to make Matt jealous, but it clearly backfires because Matt grasps my shoulders with even more enthusiasm than before.

"You HAVE to try them on," Matt says.

The girl looks us up and down. "DO either of you have eighty-nine hundred dollars?"

"HE does," Matt points to me. "He just won the lottery."

"Nice try," the girl says. "You look a little young to be a lottery winner."

"He's got the best plastic surgeon money can buy," Matt tells her.

Before the sales associate takes Matt's joke the wrong way and ushers us out of the store, I pull out my phone and show her photos of me and Jamie posing with our first installment check.

The girl smiles and takes a key from the bag clasped on her belt. "Well, in that case, you DO have to try them on."

She places the Yeezys carefully into my hands; I examine the red leather and the suede toe caps as if they're made of glass.

mint

"They're in mint condition," the clerk says. "And make a nice statement for someone who just came into a lot of cash."

posh

I step out of my Vans and gently slide my feet into the posh sneakers. They fit perfectly.

"Only two hundred pairs were made," the clerk continues. "And they sold out in eleven minutes."

I stare down at my bright red feet. "These are WAY too nice to skateboard in." I realize a small crowd has gathered, checking out the twelve-year-old looking at such a flashy pair of shoes.

flashy

"Dude, don't even think about skating in those." Matt steps next to me in the mirror and models the pristine pair of Converse Fastbreaks he's trying on. "THESE on the other hand are the perfect balance of style and functionality."

"Someone's got a great eye for footwear." The salesgirl grins at Matt. "Shall I ring these up for you?"

Matt looks to me for permission. I have to admit, I never would've even gotten the winning ticket if he didn't rope me into helping Jamie move. Buying him an awesome new pair of kicks is the least I can do, so I tell the salesgirl we'll get them.

"Great!" Then she points to my feet. "Are you ready to take those Yeezys home too?"

"You've GOT to get them," Matt says.

"My parents will KILL me if I spend nine thousand dollars on a pair of sneakers!"

"It's YOUR money, not theirs," Matt says. "If they were my size, I'D get them."

"Your friend is right," the clerk says. "They're just too fabulous NOT to get."

"Besides," Matt points out, "your dad said you had permission to buy two pairs and that's exactly what you're doing."

Through the corner of my eye I check out all the cool young men and women in the store waiting to see what I'll do. All that positive energy makes me pull out the credit card my parents finally agreed to let me have.

When I tell the clerk I'll take them, she winks and takes the card. A guy next to me gives me a thumbs-up and Matt slaps me on the back.

"I hope you don't mind if I verify this with your bank," the clerk says. "It IS a lot of money." After a moment, she turns to me and smiles. "Looks like the funds are there—and then some."

funds

As I sign the slip for the first

satchel

credit card purchase of my life, the clerk hands me our new shoes in a black satchel that looks more expensive than most of my regular sneakers. "FYI—we have a no-return policy—not that you'd ever take these back in a million years." She hands me a business card and tells me to call her the next time I want to come in. "I'd be happy to set up a private showing so you don't have to wait in line."

I love the new shoes but it's only a matter of time before I have to pay the REAL price—my parents' wrath.

I don't need to hear Mom's "peer pressure" lecture to know that my first expensive purchase with my newfound wealth might not have been the smartest decision I've ever made.

newfound

I tuck the bag under my arm with a feeling more of dread than happiness; my parents don't need to know how much these cost, do they?

JAMIE

lavish

I'VE BEEN TRYING TO KEEP MY head down and not focus on what Jamie's doing with his half of the money but it's hard not to notice his lavish lifestyle when my Instagram feed is overflowing with pictures and videos of him dropping giant amounts of cash all over town.

First, he bought a brand-new tour bus for his band. The inside is furnished like a penthouse suite—complete with private bunks, three TVs, and practically every gaming system invented. And don't get me started on the pantry filled to the brim with enough chips to make nachos for the entire planet.

furnished

I don't judge Jamie too much for indulging in this initial extravagance—considering I've only worn my nine-thousand-dollar Yeezys one afternoon since I bought them, avoiding any conversation about them with my parents.

indulging

extravagance

Jamie also bought an entire warehouse downtown where he and the other Velvet Incinerator guys can practice whenever they want without bothering any neighbors. I can't imagine what kind of luxuries he'll have in his new place.

warehouse

A wall-to-wall aquarium? His own In-N-Out Burger? An indoor pool? If that wasn't enough for his first week as a multimillionaire, he also bought Segways for each band member AND a massive SUV for himself. It's like he's a twenty-three-year-old geyser spewing money, even ordering a custom license plate with his name on it.

geyser

Since Velvet Incinerator has been on tour for this week, Jamie hasn't been home to deal with the side effects of his new status as a lottery winner being public record. Matt tells me there's been a constant barrage of press knocking on the door hoping to catch Jamie for an interview and the phone was ringing so much Matt's parents had to disconnect their landline.

interview

Meanwhile, Jamie's been posting

stories from all the world-class restaurants he's eating at on the road. Matt and I nearly barfed when we saw him slurp down a snail straight out of the shell. The French might call it "escargot," but I call it gross. Plus, every time Jamie posts himself having a fancy meal, he's with a different woman.

"You know these girls only like you because you're rich," Matt says as we FaceTime Jamie from the tour bus. "None of those supermodels would ever go out with you BEFORE you had all that money."

"So?" Even through FaceTime, Jamie's sarcasm registers loud and clear. "Also, in case you haven't noticed, Velvet Incinerator is blowing up on Spotify. Our shows are sold out weeks in advance. I COULD be getting more dates because people are finally noticing that I'm a great musician."

"Or not."

"Whatever," Jamie says. "Can you put Mom and Dad back on?"

Not long after, my mom texts that it's time to come home for dinner. Seeing how limitless Jamie's spending is compared to mine makes me lament the fact that I'm under-age and he's not. If only I didn't have to have my parents' approval on everything, especially after the sneaker fiasco. Jamie's extravagant habits motivate me to prepare a three-point presentation to convince my parents that it's time for me to splurge.

lament

splurge

"So here's what I'm thinking," I begin. "A party for my class with some entertainment."

"Great idea," Dad says. "I could strum a few tunes on that new banjo you got me. We could have a sing-along!"

I laugh politely in the hopes that Dad's only joking. "Uhm..." I stall. "I was thinking of something a bit more upscale."

upscale

"Is that another word for expensive?" Mom's tone is more curious than concerned.

"Well, I was thinking we could rent a pool at a hotel," I say cautiously.

"On a rooftop with several taco stations?" Dad asks.

"Jeremy, please!" Mom quickly shifts from curious to parental.

Dad takes a sip of his club soda. "And which famous DJ did you have in mind?"

I can't tell if Dad is purposely

trying to irritate Mom or not, but I want to finish my pitch before he does.

I scrunch up my face, anticipating their reaction. "I was thinking maybe we could hire Ariana Grande."

My dad does an actual spit take, which makes the two of us laugh. Mom, not so much.

advocates

"I'd love to know where you came up with this idea," Mom says. "A website that advocates spending college tuition on a few hours with a celebrity?"

"She's a GIANT star, Mom! Plus, she lives right here in L.A."

expenditure

"I think it's fair to say your father and I are in agreement on this expenditure." Mom turns to my dad. "Right?"

Dad makes that face he does when he knows he's about to say something that won't sit well with Mom. "It IS his money," Dad begins. "We invested so much of it already—I think if he wants to throw a star-studded bash, he's entitled."

Mom shakes her head in disbelief and I'm so grateful to Dad for deflecting some of her response away from me.

deflecting

"Maybe—and I mean MAYBE—if you were sixteen," Mom says. "But you're twelve! Absolutely not!"

I move to the second part of my presentation—an article from the *L.A. Times* and another from the *New York Times* that discuss the over-the-top bar mitzvahs kids my age are having these days.

"I'm sorry," Mom says. "Are you planning a bar mitzvah we don't know about?"

"No," I reply. "I'm just saying rich kids have parties like this all the time."

Mom actually laughs. "You're not a rich kid!"

I turn to Dad, who looks at Mom and shrugs. "He kind of is."

retreated

Before I even make it to point three, my parents have retreated to the living room, where I can hear them quietly bickering. The last thing I want is for this lottery money to come between the members of my family.

bickering

But the FIRST thing I want is a giant party with all my friends.

FINANCIAL
LANDMINES

OVER THE NEXT FEW WEEKS, IT'S hard not to notice that people treat me differently now that I suddenly have money. Even though Jamie is the one who has to deal with all the press, plenty of people around town must know we're splitting the winnings because I find myself having lots of conversations with people who never gave me the time of day before.

Jerry, the owner of the 7-Eleven that sold Jamie the ticket, now comes out from behind the counter every time I'm in the store to celebrate with a complimentary Slurpee. Business is up 300 percent since his store sold such a lucrative winning ticket. You'd think he'd use some of that extra revenue to make the Big Gulp bar a little less sticky and gross, although it's comforting there's one thing that hasn't changed with all this new money floating around.

The woman three houses down who barely smiled when I walked Bodi now pulls off her gardening gloves and talks to me over the fence like I'm her own grandson.

lucrative

revenue

Suddenly she's very interested in what I plan to study in college and what countries I'd like to travel to someday. She goes on about all the fine art there is in Europe. Last week she held me captive for almost half an hour telling me about her trip to Rome and St. Peter's Basilica.

Basilica

The same thing happens at school. I didn't mind buying Natalie a new phone, getting Peter more followers, or helping Abby rescue those dogs, but I didn't envision the feeling of weirdness lingering in the air afterward.

envision

Everyone seems much nicer to me, but I feel like more of an outsider than ever before. Instead of including me in conversations about homework or shows we watched last night, my classmates

lingering

just want to hear about what I'm BUYING. Peter even had a viewing party for his latest YouTube videos at his dad's condo over the weekend. When I asked why he didn't invite me, he said he didn't think I was into that kind of thing anymore.

I can't tell if the problem stems from my friends or from me. Are they acting weird because they feel they owe me something now? Or am I creating a problem where there isn't one? I thought money was supposed to make people feel good—not annoyingly self-conscious.

This windfall—for which I am totally grateful—is shedding light on aspects of my relationships with my friends that I never used to think about before. I decide to give my brain a break from this new confusion with some good old-fashioned video games. I settle onto my bed with my laptop, but when I open the Internet browser I see an email from the extreme sports supply company where I ordered my skateboard park. The backyard system I bought is still on back order and the delivery is postponed another two weeks.

It's not that I mind skateboarding at the regular park—duh!—it's just that Matt, Dad, and I spent hours coming up with the perfect configuration for our backyard.

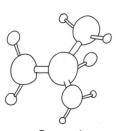

configuration

The company blames the delay on a shortage of the high-density plastic, which makes me wonder how plastic can be delayed when it's pretty much everywhere—including the 3D printer next to my desk. Hey,

density

why wait for a custom skate park to be delivered when I can PRINT one? I pick up one of my self-designed Derek action figures and make him do a backflip off the top of the machine. The truth is, it took hours for the printer to produce one action figure. It would take MONTHS to render an entire skate park, and I don't even want to think about how much filament it would use. I guess it's faster and cheaper to be patient.

render

I take a deep breath to keep myself from getting frustrated. Am I getting angry that my custom skateboard park is delayed?

Who Am I?

I take a few more breaths, bring Bodi up on my bed, and email the company that the delay is fine.

MORE
OPPORTUNITIES

I THINK ABOUT TRYING TO BRIBE
Ms. McCoddle with some cash to get
me out of this afternoon's history
test, then realize that will probably
only get me into MORE trouble.

bribe

When I get to study hall, there's
an older kid I've seen around who
keeps opening and closing his book
like an accordion. If he's trying to
get Mr. Bernard's attention, it's not

working; the teacher scrolls through his phone without even looking up.

After I take the seat beside him, the kid introduces himself as Rio. "You're the zillionaire, right? You done any investing yet?"

investing

"My parents have had lots of meetings with money experts, but I haven't done anything myself."

Rio leans toward me in his chair and whispers, which isn't necessary since Mr. Bernard doesn't seem to care what we do. "My dad made a bundle investing in cat cafés," Rio says. "He tripled his money in a few months."

"REALLY?" I've seen a few of those cafés around the city, but since I'm more of a dog person and don't drink coffee, I never thought about visiting one. I tell Rio I'll definitely talk to my parents about it.

"You should have kids here at school pitch you ideas," Rio continues. "Lots of kids are doing start-ups these days."

"Like who?" This guy is a thousand times more plugged into what's going on around here than I am.

He starts counting off kids I don't know on his fingers. "Renee is monetizing her TikTok, Bobby C is interning for a big YouTube guy..."

"Doesn't interning mean you DON'T get paid?" I ask.

"He'll get paid in the long term, learning the best social media stuff from a big shot." Rio snaps his fingers. "Kids are moving and shaking, especially in L.A." He holds up his phone. "You should have as many followers as other billionaires—you've got to get with the program!"

He goes back to flapping the cover of his book back and forth. This time, Mr. Bernard looks up and orders Rio to keep it down.

"Here's what you should do," Rio whispers. "If you gave me, let's say, two thousand dollars, I can give it to my Dad to invest in the cat café and in a few months you'll have six thousand dollars—guaranteed!"

It's not figuring out the math that stops me in my tracks; it's the word *guaranteed*. I don't know much about growing money, but I DO know when you roll the dice with a start-up, making a ton of money back isn't a surefire thing. "What's the name of the cat café?" I ask.

surefire

The question catches him off guard. "Uhm...Meow Meow?"

I take out my textbook and tell him I've got to study for my test.

I'd rather flunk Ms. McCoddle's class than invest in a business called Meow Meow.

AN UNEXPECTED DELIVERY

unload

WHEN THE SKATEBOARD PARK FI-nally comes, it takes the delivery person twelve trips to unload all the giant boxes out of the truck. I run inside to tell Dad the purchase I've been waiting for all month is finally here.

The UPS guy hands his keypad scanner to Dad for his signature, but Dad shakes his head and points to me. I feel like a real grown-up as I write my name with the stylus across the screen. I am in charge of my own destiny!

stylus

Dad slices the biggest box open with the tiny knife I used to be obsessed with that he still keeps on his key chain. I hand the scanner back to the UPS guy and ask when someone will be coming by to assemble all the different parts of the skateboard park.

The man scrolls through the shipment details on the screen and shrugs. "Did you order this kit with assembly?"

I suddenly no longer feel like a competent adult but like a kid who didn't read the instructions all the way through.

Dad and I go inside and look up

the order online in my browsing history. He points to one of the options available at checkout. "Expert assembly—additional two thousand dollars."

I look at the box, unchecked. "Maybe they'll let me add installation now," I say.

installation

Dad suggests I call the customer service number on the bottom of the page. Usually I'll do anything to avoid making an old-fashioned phone call, but I'm eager to get this skateboard park up and running. I'm glad Dad doesn't mention anything about the two thousand dollars; he's probably thinking that's a lot of money—and it IS—but I don't think either of us wants to open this can of worms with Mom.

After being on hold for a few

minutes, I read the woman on the other end of the phone my order number and ask when she can send someone out here.

She lets out a low whistle and tells me the bad news. Since I didn't request the installation when I ordered the unit, the company won't be able to coordinate one for me now.

Dad motions for me to put the phone on speaker so he can join in, but even his sympathetic appeal does nothing to change the results.

appeal

"Well," Dad says after I hang up, "we can look for someone on Craigslist or call a local handyman."

I can tell by the way Dad rubs his chin that he's remembering the last time we hired someone from Craigslist to help with some carpentry around the house. It took

carpentry

shoddy

posit

more than a month to find someone with enough references, and even then the guy did such a shoddy job that it took another month to find someone to fix what the first guy had wrecked.

I tell Dad there's no way I'm waiting two months to break in this skate park.

"Might I posit a suggestion?" Dad holds open the back door and gestures to the driveway full of boxes. "How about if WE put it together?"

"US?!" I shout. "I can barely help you when that section of the fence always falls down."

"We already have a contact in customer service if we get stuck," Dad replies.

"She'd do a better job than I would," I say.

"It comes with a pretty detailed installation manual." Dad pulls part of a ramp from the open box. "How about we give it a try? If it's hopeless, we'll hire someone immediately."

"Can we just assume it's hopeless and call someone now?" I ask. "This is a massive construction project— it'll take us forever!"

I know Dad's trying to be a good father and connect with me—but he might as well be suggesting that we demolish our bathroom and build an outhouse on the roof. However, the look on his face is filled with such affection and childlike curiosity that I cave and tell him okay.

There's no room for Mom's car

outhouse

when she pulls up, so she parks on the street in front of the house. "I'm guessing the skateboard park is finally here?" she calls from the mailbox.

"Yes," Dad answers. "And WE'RE the ones putting it together."

document

"I LOVE that idea!" Mom claps her hands together. "I'll document the entire process on video. Speaking of things to document, look what came today: Derek's first credit card statement." She holds up a thick envelope from the bank with my name on it. "Now you can learn how to pay your bills."

"I have to build my own skate park AND pay my own bills too?" I shout. "How is it that I'm suddenly rich and have MORE work to do?"

"Relax." Mom drops the envelope

into my hands and pats me on the back. "We'll just look over the charges, make sure there aren't any duplicates or fraud, and pay online. Easy as pie."

duplicates

I tear open the envelope and unfold the pages inside.

Mom peers over my shoulder and guides me down the list. "There's the charge for the new wheelchair that's coming, the Apple store, animal shelter..."

"The skate park." I point to the charge from the extreme sports company.

"Jeez; it really adds up, doesn't it?"

I can see the wheels in Mom's head spin as she mentally tallies how much money I've already gone through. When she flips to the second page, she yanks the

paper cut

clutches

statement out of my hands so fast I get a paper cut.

"Ten thousand dollars at a SNEAKER STORE?" She looks up at me. "We agreed you would only get two pairs!"

"I DID get two pairs." I slouch onto the grass. "And one wasn't even for me. I let Matt pick out a pair too."

Mom still clutches the statement with both hands as she lowers it away from her face and takes a deep breath. "Matt's family has their own half of the winnings. You can't let him pressure you into spending thousands of dollars on him."

"He didn't," I respond. "His pair only cost two hundred."

Dad leans on the doorframe and shakes his head. "Are you saying you spent over nine thousand dollars on one pair of shoes?"

Mom sets her sights on Dad. "You were supposed to be supervising! You know those retail associates work on commission!"

supervising

The only thing worse than watching my parents argue is watching them argue about something I did. "I asked Dad to drop us off down the block so we could go in by ourselves," I say. "And...yeah." My eyes sink to the floor. "I spent eighty-nine hundred dollars—plus tax—on one pair of sneakers."

Mom grabs the sides of her head. "How on earth could a pair of sneakers be worth that much?!"

"These aren't just ANY sneakers!" I point to my feet.

My sales pitch obviously has no effect on Mom. After what seems like forever, she uncrosses her arms. "Derek, you're twelve years old."

"Don't remind me."

"What I mean is," she continues, "you—and your feet—aren't finished growing yet. You just wasted a good chunk of your winnings on designer sneakers that won't even fit you next year."

She heads inside, but not before taking one more glance at my shoes. "They look like overpriced clown shoes to me."

I follow Mom into the house to pay my first credit card bill, feeling more like a bozo than a big shot.

PASS THE ELBOW GREASE

IT'S HARD TO COMPLAIN ABOUT spending your Saturday doing chores when the only task on your list is building yourself a skate park. I've barely even made my toast— one smothered in peanut butter, the other in avocado—when Dad throws me a pair of leather work gloves.

smothered

referring

"I printed out the instruction manual so we don't have to keep referring back to a screen in the hot sun." He tosses me a document fastened with a large clip; the manual is the size of my math textbook.

"We are NEVER going to be able to do this ourselves," I tell him for what seems like the millionth time. "Maybe we should just start looking for a carpenter."

"Where's the fun in that?" Dad motions for me to follow him outside.

stomp

The first thing we do is unpack the six boxes that contain the sections that form the base. I'm about to stomp on the boxes so they'll fit into the recycling bin until

I realize I'm wearing my Yeezys and don't want to scuff them up. (Taking care of expensive things takes SO MUCH effort.) If Dad notices my hesitation, he thankfully doesn't say anything.

It takes us almost an hour to lay out the foundation of the bowl, and another forty-five minutes to locate the specific screws, bolts, and washers inside the giant plastic bag of hardware. I don't mind the work; between the sunshine and the Beatles playing in the background, it isn't a bad way to spend a Saturday morning.

reacquaint

It takes a few minutes to reacquaint myself with Dad's cordless drill; I haven't used it since I helped him hang bookshelves in the living

cordless

bidirectional

unproductive

resin

room a few years ago. The drill is bidirectional, which means the bit can go forward and backward to take screws out as well as put them in.

It's fun to make the drill push the screw into the hard plastic, then reverse it and pull it out. (Needless to say Dad stops me from this unproductive activity pretty quickly.)

By the time Mom opens the kitchen window and asks if we want lunch, the resin base of the skateboard park is together and secure.

"I was worried this model might be too small," I say.

"I was worried it was going to be too big," Dad adds.

But there's room to walk around the large base, with most of the yard still remaining accessible. Sweaty and proud, we head inside for sandwiches.

"We're done for today, right?" I ask Dad.

"If you call one tenth of the job done, then I guess we are."

I look over to see if he's angry but Dad just smiles. "We can try to bang out some more this weekend, or take our time," he says. "Your call."

On the one hand, all these ramps and jumps make me want to spend the rest of the afternoon skateboarding. On the other hand, working alongside Dad building something substantial seems like a good way to enjoy the weekend too.

substantial

"How about if we do a little more," I suggest, "and plan out tomorrow too?"

"Sounds good to me." Dad cuts his grilled cheese in half and takes a giant bite.

It's kind of a perfect day.

PARTY TIME!

AFTER WAY MORE CONVERSATIONS than are necessary, Mom finally relents and agrees to let me have a giant party. Ariana Grande is out— which is too bad because every single girl in my school would've gone NUTS. (Maybe I should've researched if Greta Thunberg sings. She might be an even bigger draw.)

Mom suggests we rent Darcy's

house, where we stayed during the Malibu fires, but Darcy has relatives visiting for a few months, so we can't. We call lots of hotels, including the Roosevelt. The pool's not on the roof, but a famous artist named David Hockney painted a mural on the bottom of it so it's this iconic piece of L.A. history, which I doubt will impress any of my friends. The hotel has been around since 1927—it hosted the first Academy Awards— and is a real celebrity hangout, so when they have an available Saturday afternoon and evening, I decide to stop calling around and host the party there.

mural

Mom suggests we invite the whole class so no one will feel left out. I don't admit I was planning to do that anyway but for a different reason. (Is it bad I want to show off my new wealth just a LITTLE bit?)

I feel strange inviting everyone without including Ms. McCoddle, so she says she'll stop by and say hello sometime during the party.

My parents insist the invitations state *no gifts*. I tell them since it isn't my birthday no one will bring gifts anyway but Mom doesn't want my friends to feel obligated. It takes me a while to understand her argument.

"Wait?" I ask. "Does that mean just 'cuz I have money now, I never get presents again—ever? What about Christmas and my birthday?"

Mom laughs. "Of course we'll still get you presents. It makes us happy!"

I'm not entirely reassured. "But what about from my friends?"

"I can't speak for them," Mom says. "But right now, let's just finalize these invitations."

finalize

When we arrive at the hotel on the day of the party, a woman named Kim introduces herself to us as soon as we get there and says her job is to make sure my party is 100 percent awesome. She has the whitest teeth and the shortest skirt I've ever seen. Kim shows us around the pool with its famous mural but I'm more interested in the super-cool daybeds and cabanas my friends, classmates, and I will be hanging out in all day.

cabanas

discreetly

Kim must've discreetly motioned for the rest of the hotel staff, because suddenly we're surrounded by eight servers in matching orange outfits. Kim gives us the rundown on the two taco stations, snow-cone bar, dessert buffet, and temporary tattoo parlor. The surface of the pool is covered with giant floaties and rafts.

She introduces us to the DJ who works all their celebrity parties. He seems like a nice guy but definitely not as impressive as Ariana Grande would've been. (Thanks again, Mom.)

Kim scrolls through her phone. "It's a perfect eighty-two degrees without a cloud in the sky—you and your friends have fun!"

Matt and Carly arrive together and are the first to show up, followed soon after by Umberto and his brother Eduardo.

I tell Matt he doesn't need to

pollen

stockpile the tacos because the servers will be refilling the stations all afternoon.

Carly is obsessed with green smoothies and requests every add-in on the menu, including bee pollen, which makes no sense at all. Eduardo helps Umberto into the pool, where I'm guessing Umberto—who's half fish—will spend most of the day.

"I've got to build some arm muscle before the extreme wheelchair arrives!" Umberto shouts as he completes a lap. "Those ramp flips take serious upper body strength."

I invited fifty kids and everyone is here except Abby, who's visiting her grandparents out of town.

"The music is loud, the water is warm, and the smoothies are cold."

Dad settles himself into one of the daybeds next to Mom, who's already enjoying the sun with a stack of magazines.

"I haven't worn this bathing suit in years," Mom says. "That exercise bike you got me is a godsend, Derek."

The lifeguard seems pretty low-key as she keeps track of everyone yakking and swimming in the pool. She and Umberto are talking about *Stranger Things* as he takes a break from his workout on the giant swan raft.

limbo

"Hey," Matt says. "Kim says we can set up the limbo bar."

Leave it to Matt to find who's in charge of activities and see what's available. The DJ immediately

fleece

switches to limbo music and half of the pool climbs out to play.

As the afternoon progresses into early evening, the firepits magically ignite and piles of the softest fleece blankets I've ever felt appear on all the daybeds. I'm about to tell Mom I'm glad she suggested this place when I overhear someone panicking by the juice bar.

"My phone! I can't find my phone!"

I turn to see Natalie frantically lifting up several beach towels. "I JUST got it and now it's gone!"

"I'm sure it's here somewhere," Carly tells her. "Hold on, I'll call it for you." She reaches under the beach chair into her bag. "That's weird..." She frowns. "Mine's missing too."

A few of my classmates retreat from the tacos and snow cones to safeguard their belongings; I hear several more outcries of distress when other classmates can't find their phones either. Mom hands me mine, which she made me stash in her purse so I wouldn't accidentally jump in the pool with it still in my pocket—again. "Ask the DJ to turn down the music first, then call Carly's phone and see if we hear it."

safeguard

As I sprint to the DJ table, I spot something fishy: Peter filming himself as he runs to the private changing room with something heavy bundled in a towel. "HEY!" I shout.

bundled

Peter stops filming and freezes in place. I don't have to ask what he's got in that towel—the guilt on his face tells me everything I need to know.

I bolt toward him and he takes off at full speed for the changing room. Luckily, what I lack in study skills I more than make up for in agility. I kick into high gear and quickly close the gap between us to block him from the changing room door.

altercation

"Put down the towel," I say.

Peter starts taping our altercation. "No can do."

"Come on," I command. "We're trying to have a good time. There's no reason to prank everybody by taking their phones."

"Easy for you to say," Peter answers. "You're a rich kid now. The rest of us need to find other ways to stand out. I'm building a following by punking people." He turns around and makes a break for the lobby.

punking

"MATT, CATCH HIM!" I yell.

"What?" Matt looks up at me with a mouthful of taco.

"HE'S GOT THE PHONES!" I point to Peter dashing past the daybeds.

Matt takes off toward Peter and gets close enough to throw his plate at Peter's legs. Peter slows down and it's all the time I need to catch up. I grab ahold of the bundle and try to pull it away, but his grip is too tight.

"You're being ridiculous," I shout. "Give back the phones."

"What's going on here?" Dad asks as he makes his way over.

Peter tugs back the towel, then holds it high in the air.

I try to grab it but Peter yanks so hard, we both lose our balance. I knock over the recycling bin, sending two glass bottles crashing onto the cement, while Peter stumbles backward and slips on the rest of Matt's taco.

The entire party gasps as nine phones fly into the air like fireworks in slow motion. Everyone shouts as all the phones land in the pool.

The lifeguard blows her whistle. "Everyone out!"

The DJ stops the music with a giant record screech and I know my party is officially a bust.

The orange-clad pool attendants get to work cleaning the broken glass and cordoning off the pool. I can't look anyone in the eyes as my classmates dry off and get ready to leave. Mom and Dad use their phones to help kids call their parents, assuring them we'll pay for replacements—which of course means I'LL pay for replacements.

Umberto stops alongside the daybed where I'm sitting with my head in my hands. "If it makes you feel any better, I had a great time!"

"Thanks," I say without looking up.

Peter holds up his arms in victory as he leaves. "Thanks for the footage, bro. I've already gotten two hundred likes!"

footage

The next person to approach me is Kim, only this time she left her brilliant smile behind. "You've actually set a new hotel record." She hands me a stack of papers thicker than a book report. "This is the largest bill I've seen for an event that didn't include alcohol."

I flip to the last page to see how much this disaster of a party is costing me. In addition to the entertainment, buffets, and gratuity, they've listed an $18,000 service fee. "What is the eighteen thousand dollars for?!"

gratuity

aspiring

"Because of the phones and broken glass, we have to drain and refill the pool." She seems almost as sad as I am, which makes me realize she's probably also an aspiring actress. "We have to reimburse our other guests tomorrow for not having use of the pool, so that's another ten thousand dollars."

penalties

Even with both my parents trying to talk her out of these penalties, Kim doesn't budge. In the end, I'm forced to hand over my new credit card.

As I sign my name at the bottom of the bill, I wouldn't wish winning a billion dollars on my worst enemy.

NEW STUFF FOR SCHOOL

pledge

EVEN THOUGH THE PARTY—AND Peter—cost me a small fortune, I can't go back on the pledge I made myself to donate a new media center to the school. Umberto and I spend several weeks doing research on various kinds of equipment. He's a whiz at knowing the best kind of tablets and styluses to get. He's already read all the reviews on the latest drawing, animation, and video editing software, which simplifies the whole process. We order a green screen, ring lights, and several digital video cameras, as well as eight new computers loaded with top-of-the-line graphics and coding software.

$$\frac{4}{8} = \frac{1}{2}$$

simplifies

It's been a while since I took the after-school class, so my coding is a bit rusty, but Umberto's continued to hone his skills—so much that he even did some coding for his mom's company over winter break.

hone

"The question is, where are we going to PUT all this?" Umberto asks. "The equipment takes up a lot of space; I don't think Ms. Myer's going to be happy with losing half the library."

It's a question I've been wondering about too. We both turn to Principal Demetri.

"Since we combined two of the sixth-grade classes last year, there's an extra classroom that used to be Ms. Rutt's," Principal Demetri explains. "I think we can set up the new media lab in there."

We follow Demetri down the hall and wait while he rummages through the giant key ring that's been jangling in his pocket. "It's a little stale from being closed up all year, but once we air it out I think it'll be fine."

jangling

I tell the principal this room will be more than fine and begin to open the windows. All of the other students are long gone for the day but Umberto and I spend the next hour laying out where the different media stations will go once the new gear arrives.

Demetri directs us to rearrange the desks and tables in an open configuration. "This is a good design for collaborating." Principal Demetri puts his hands on his hips, taking in the new setup. I want to ask if he's okay since he's out of breath and profusely sweating, but I don't want to make it look like he's too out of shape to move a few chairs and desks.

"We're going to call this the Derek Fallon Media Lab." Demetri raises his arms as if he's holding a large neon sign. "This school never could've afforded such state-of-the-art technology without you."

I tell Principal Demetri that I

appreciate the gesture but just calling it the media lab is fine.

After we close the windows and secure the building, Umberto sidles up beside me. "Why don't you want your name on it?" he asks. "It's a real tribute."

Sally Williams
1939 – 2020
BEST MOM EVER

tribute

"That's easy for you to say," I tell Umberto. "You're a good student with killer grades. I can barely keep up around here." Out of the corner of my eye I watch Bill's van approaching, so I have less than a minute to blurt out how I feel. "It's not like I deserve it."

"You TOTALLY deserve it!" When Umberto wheels in front of me, his expression is full of kindness. "You're donating a ton of money to help kids at this school learn new skills."

I shake my head. "It's not like I earned the money."

"Nobody earns a lottery! You got a gift and you're paying it forward—that's a good thing." He gestures for Bill to wait. "No—it's a GREAT thing! Whether you want your name on the lab is one thing, but acting like you didn't do something good here? That is unacceptable, my friend." Umberto stares at me, waiting for some kind of response.

"I'm just ... not that good at a lot of things," I finally answer.

"I disagree." Umberto wheels his chair over to Bill, who's got the van's ramp ready to go. "You're good at being generous and funny and loyal." Umberto ascends the motorized platform as he talks. "You're good at

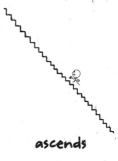

ascends

wallowing

being Derek Fallon—and that's good enough for me."

Leave it to Umberto to keep me from wallowing in self-pity after finding a pot of gold at the end of the lottery rainbow.

Just as they're about to drive off, Umberto rolls down the window. "Hey, when's my new wheelchair coming?"

I laugh and yell after him that it's being delivered next week. There's nothing like a good friend to help you keep things in perspective.

DOG BED BLUES

WHEN I GET HOME, I'M DISAP-pointed to see that someone—I'm guessing Mom—has placed Bodi's new mink dog bed outside with the trash barrels. I drag it back into the house where it belongs.

"You didn't have to get rid of it," I tell my mom. She's working at the table with a calculator and a stack of bills.

calculator

"I wasn't the one who brought it out there." She looks up at me from over the top of her reading glasses. "Bodi did."

I drop the dog bed by Bodi lying underneath the table. "Are you telling me Bodi dragged this outside by himself?"

"Maybe he didn't want to sleep on top of an animal who was killed for its skin. What—you think that mink walked into a dog bed factory and said, 'Please kill me and take my fur'?"

As if to prove Mom's point, Bodi grabs the mink bed with his teeth and drags it to the back door. I shake my head and reluctantly hold the door open for him.

Mom looks at me and laughs. "Maybe you can make a pillow out of it for your bed."

I slump my elbows down on the counter next to her.

She sets down her pen and gives me her full attention. "I know you wanted to get Bodi something special. I'm sure he knows that too."

"I should've just gotten him those salmon treats he likes from Trader Joe's." Through the window I watch Bodi haul the costly bedding to the curb.

I rummage through the pantry, finally settling on a bag of dried apricots, which means it's definitely time for some grocery shopping. "You know, we could order food from one of those delivery services," I suggest. "So you never have to go to the store again."

Mom doesn't even look up from her paperwork. "I like picking out my

apricots

lilies

receipts

own produce and flowers—I could never leave that to somebody else." She motions to the vase of lilies and tulips on the counter.

"You could get fresh flowers delivered every day," I say. "We could set that up right now." I hold up my phone to demonstrate my point.

Mom leans back in her chair and asks if I know what she's doing. I look at the table full of receipts and papers and ask her if she's paying bills.

"Yes," she answers. "And how on earth are you going to learn how to do this if you just order each and every thing you want without planning or budgeting for it?"

"How can you possibly budget eighteen thousand dollars to empty a pool!"

Mom smiles. "You don't—but you've heard that saying 'Save it for a rainy day'? Draining that pool was YOUR rainy day—hopefully the last one for a while."

I can hear Dad upstairs on his phone and pray he comes down here soon to bail me out. It's bad enough I have to eat dried apricots, but I have to listen to another one of Mom's teaching moments too?

"I actually like doing a monthly check-in to see what money I have coming in and going out," Mom continues. "Even with millions coming in, you need to keep track of what's going out too."

I can't tell if she just glanced down at my Yeezys.

Finally Dad shuffles into the room, finished with his call.

"I was just explaining to Derek how it's important to keep track of income and expenditures," Mom says.

As Dad scoots to the sink his face is blocked by the cupboard door so Mom can't see him. He gives me a look that says, *I got this*.

"Anything we can do to help you wrap up this work?" Dad asks. "I hear Boggle calling." He gestures for me to follow him to the living room, where we collapse in front of the TV.

"I bet you didn't think there'd be so many life lessons attached to that lottery ticket," Dad says.

"It's definitely not as easy as I thought it would be. Even with Bodi!" I fill Dad in on my ungrateful mutt as he grabs Boggle from the shelf.

ungrateful

"How can I work when my two favorite people in the world are waiting to get their butts kicked?" Mom hands Dad a glass of wine and sits beside him.

After three straight losses I head to bed and am relieved to see Bodi follow me upstairs. There's nothing worse than a dog harboring a grudge.

harboring

The next morning I'm surprised to find Dad curled up on the couch with a pillow and one of the quilts from the linen closet.

Were my parents fighting because of me? Is the money driving a wedge between them?

wedge

I tiptoe into the kitchen, where Mom's back at the table with her bills, this time with coffee. "Are things okay with you and Dad?" I slip two unwrapped Pop-Tarts into the toaster. "Are you guys arguing about how I should spend the money again?"

Mom makes a face like she doesn't know what I'm talking about. When I point to the couch in the next room, she smiles. "Red wine always makes your dad snore," she says. "I should've thought of that when I brought him a glass last night. He had the decency to sleep down here, which I appreciate since I've got a full day today."

A wave of relief washes over me as I put my waffles on the plate. "I just wouldn't want you and Dad to be fighting...you know...over something like money."

Mom seems confused. "Derek, don't you think our family is stronger than that? I don't care if you give every last penny away. Your dad and I might disagree on how you spend your winnings—as we said before, this is new territory for all of us— but we're certainly not going to let it come between us."

Dad stumbles into the kitchen and heads for the coffeepot. "You up for finishing the skate park this weekend?"

When I tell him I can't think of anything I'd rather do, I mean it.

HOW MUCH MONEY?

cramming

MATT AND I ARE CRAMMING FOR our test before math when I feel him staring at me.

"Jamie's in a ton of trouble," he says. "Since he's twenty-three, he has control of his own winnings, but when my parents found out how much money he's burned through, they went ballistic!"

Maybe—finally!—Jamie will have

to deal with the same kinds of restrictions I have. I ask Matt how much money his brother's already spent.

dismay

Matt shakes his head in dismay, then can't help but laugh. "Close to six million dollars."

"WHAT?!" My math notes scatter onto the floor of the

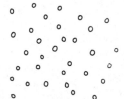

scatter

hallway outside class. "It's literally impossible to go through that much money so fast!"

"Apparently not for Jamie," Matt says. "He's got multiple restaurant and bar bills for ten thousand dollars EACH. I bet most of it was to impress girls," he adds.

I nod in agreement, not mentioning how I wanted to hire Ariana Grande to sing at my party for that exact reason.

"He also sank a million dollars in some cat café," Matt continues. "Who would EVER invest in a business called Meow Meow?"

"Six million dollars." I let out a low whistle. "I guess it IS a good thing we took the money in installments. Can you imagine if he just blew through half a billion dollars?"

Mr. Morelli calls us in to start, but as I stare at the math problems all I can think about is how right my parents were about trying to be smart with my winnings.

After bombing the test, I head to the cafeteria, where I run into Umberto IN HIS NEW WHEELCHAIR.

"Dude," he shouts. "It came this morning, that's why I'm late. You've got to check this out!"

He shows me the Spinergy X-laced

wheels and the rear air shocks—both massive improvements on his regular chair. "And look at the front lip on the footrest. It's shaped just like a skateboard so I can launch down a ramp." He zooms down the hall and calls over his shoulder, "Race you!"

launch

He zips around two younger kids, who jump out of the way just in time. I sprint after Umberto but even at top speed I can't catch up.

"You're the fastest kid in this school!" I shout after him.

He hangs a tight left toward the science labs and I charge after him.

"What is going on here?!" Principal Demetri booms. "There's no running in the halls."

We skid to a halt to face the principal. I'm doubled over, catching my breath while Umberto is still cool as a cucumber.

"Technically, I wasn't running," Umberto answers.

"Is that supposed to be funny?" Demetri asks.

I tell our principal that Umberto just got a cool new wheelchair and I was helping him test it out.

unsafe

"You both were being unsafe and inconsiderate of other students."

I'm surprised how angry he is given that we spent an afternoon with him last week setting up the new media lab.

Principal Demetri points to me. "This isn't your first offense, Derek. I reprimanded you and Matt for the same thing last month. And you"— he shifts his focus to Umberto—

"that chair is too dangerous for school property. Consider this a formal warning."

"But I just got it!" Umberto says. "I'll refrain from any extreme stunts at school, I promise."

Demetri points down the hall to his office. "I can't have students running wild and racing BMXs down the halls. If I catch either of you doing this again, it'll be suspension."

"WHAT?!" Umberto's mouth hangs open.

"You're threatening us with suspension?" I ask. "I just funded a whole new media lab! Every student will benefit and I'm in trouble for running down the hallway?"

benefit

Principal Demetri must've gotten a flat tire on the way to school to

infraction

preferential

altruism

be this angry over such a small infraction. I change tactics and lower my voice, which will hopefully give him a chance to calm down.

"Derek Fallon, if you think you'll get preferential treatment because you made a donation to this school, you are very much mistaken," he says. "The school appreciates your altruism, but that doesn't mean you are exempt from its rules."

I wait until Principal Demetri is down the hall to apologize to Umberto, but when I turn to him he's wearing a huge grin.

"Dude, that was incredible!" He slaps my arm. "I can't believe I got in trouble for racing down the hall! This is the best day ever!"

While I don't agree, I can see

where he's coming from. "Congratulations, Umberto. Welcome to the wonderful world of being one warning away from getting kicked out of school."

I BUILD SOMETHING BIG

illegible

WHEN THE WEEKEND ROLLS around, Dad can't wait to get started on the skateboard park. I'm still buttering toast but he's got the instruction manual laid across the kitchen table, marked up with notes in his illegible handwriting. Mom's got a full day of patients lined up and can't document our progress, so I text Matt to come over. Once he hears that power tools are involved, he's here within the hour.

"I know my job is to film this, but I get to wear a tool belt, right?" he asks.

We only have one; Dad, however, happily obliges and hands Matt the tool belt he's wearing. Matt buckles it around his waist and tucks his phone into one of the compartments.

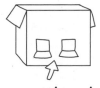

compartments

"Is today the day we finish this Herculean task?" Dad turns to me expectantly.

Herculean

I scan the backyard, covered with ramps, boxes, and bags of hardware. There's still a lot to be done but the base of the skateboard park is sturdy and ready for other pieces to be attached. "We might need tomorrow too." I throw Bodi a tennis ball, which he ignores.

"It takes what it takes," Dad says. It's one of those quotes that grown-ups say—Ms. McCoddle says it too—but I'm not really sure what it means. I wonder if people only say it to kids like me who take more time than others to finish certain tasks. I decide not to dwell on it and help Dad find the pieces of the side bowl the manual tells us to install next.

As cool as it is to film the whole adventure, Matt can't deny the urge to help in the construction and eventually joins in. He alternates between filming and assisting Dad in keeping the sections straight while I fasten them with the drill. Every time I try to give the more difficult jobs to Dad, he shakes his head and tells me he's here to assist ME, not the other way around. He also keeps reminding us to drink water so we don't get dehydrated. I know this also means Bodi, so I go inside to refill his water bowl too.

dehydrated

When we break for lunch, I'm disappointed that after all that work, we've only finished one side of the bowl.

"You SURE you don't want to hire someone to finish it?" Matt asks once my father's gone inside. "There's no shame in building HALF a skateboard park."

I tell him I was thinking the same thing—especially since my bank account—unlike Jamie's—is still pretty substantial.

"You could even hire a CREW," Matt continues. "Knock this out in a day and use it tomorrow."

whistling

I gesture for Matt to check out my dad through the kitchen window. "He's WHISTLING," I say. "He LOVES this—I want to try to finish what we started."

What I don't tell Matt is that I really want to see this project to the end too. I don't know how to explain it, but all the weirdness that has accompanied my new wealth has

unmoored

left me feeling a little unmoored, and doing something concrete with my own hands has actually made things easier for me, not harder.

A few minutes later, Dad comes out with a tray of turkey-cheese-and-tomato sandwiches along with

devour

a pitcher of ice water. We devour the food, then get back to work.

With the days getting longer, there's enough light to work until

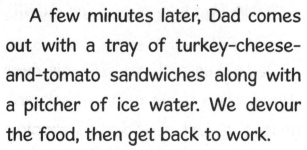

almost eight. When we get hungry around dinnertime, I'm the one who goes in to make the sandwiches so we can keep plugging away. I'm shocked Matt's still here; this is the longest I've seen him also fully engaged in a project.

engaged

By the time it's almost too dark to tell a screw from a washer, Dad points to the last section and asks if we're up for finishing. Matt takes out his cell and tapes me screwing in the final ramp as Dad leans against the piece to hold it down.

"OMG," Matt shouts. "You did it!"

"WE did it," I respond.

Dad takes pictures with his own phone, then turns on the backyard floodlights just as Mom is wrapping up her day next door.

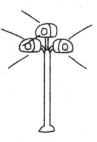

floodlights

"Job well done!" She pulls out her

phone and takes several photos of
Matt, Dad, and me standing inside
the backyard bowl.

"There's one last step," Dad says.
For a moment I think we forgot a
bolt or washer, then I realize what
he means.

"Time to skate!" Matt and I grab
our decks from the driveway and
race into my new skateboard park.

tentatively

Both my parents take videos of
Matt and me testing out the ramps—
first tentatively, then confidently.
Mr. Drake next door comes by to
see what all the commotion is about
and I immediately worry that our
wheels are making too much noise.
My fears are put to rest when he
flashes us a big smile and a thumbs-
up.

I'm sure if Dad and I had hired

someone to build this park, these initial runs would still be pretty sweet. But I also think they're a bit more satisfying because we built this on our own.

FRANKLY SPEAKING

WHEN I CALL THE FOUNDATION that trains capuchins, I leave a message for Mary—the director who came to remove Frank from our house last year. She calls me back the next day and gives me an update on how Frank's doing.

"He's helping a wonderful young woman named Julie who's got

cerebral palsy. Frank and Julie took to each other immediately."

I tell myself this is good news—no, great news—for both Julie and Frank. But to be completely honest, a tiny part of me is jealous too. "Did she watch the video I made of Frank's favorite things? Watching Westerns? Baby carrots?"

"Yes, Julie found that very helpful," Mary says. "It seems Frank's recently developed an affinity for anime—he and Julie are obsessed!"

affinity

"Anime?!" I shout, then lower my voice to regular volume. "I had no idea." *Did Frank always like anime? I wonder. Or did this interest begin with Julie?*

I finally get around to the main

purpose of my call and tell Mary I'd like to donate to their nonprofit.

"We will certainly appreciate that!" she answers. "We run totally on donations, so every dollar counts."

When I mention the dollar amount I'm thinking about, Mary is

uncharacteristically

uncharacteristically quiet.

"Why, Derek," she finally says. "A donation of that size would be astounding! What an act of

astounding

philanthropy!"

For some reason, I've pictured handing her one of those giant checks while all the capuchins—Frank

philanthropy

included—jump around the room in celebration. I ask her about delivering the money in person and getting to see Frank at the same time.

"Oh, that won't be possible,"

Mary says. "We never let former foster family members visit their capuchins once they're placed with someone permanently."

She must feel my disappointment through the phone because she immediately continues.

"It would be too confusing for Frank, or any animal," she says. "We don't want to disorient him while he's settling in with someone new."

In my mind, I COMPLETELY understand what she's saying but I'm also thinking, *I'm about to give you half a million dollars—can't you make an exception?* I don't say it out loud, of course, but we both know I COULD.

exception

"I hope you're not too dis-appointed," Mary says. "We'd love you to visit our facility and meet some of the other capuchins."

I assure her that I'll still donate to her organization, but in this case, I'll probably mail a check instead—especially since one of my grandmother's friends is undergoing chemotherapy and Grammy is tied up for the next few months.

"Derek, we appreciate your generosity so much," Mary responds. "Please do stop in the next time you're in town to see your grandmother."

I tell Mary I will and hang up, a little sad but happy Frank is doing well.

This is another situation where winning the lottery made things kind of weird. I'm figuring out that having this much money changes

the dynamic between people—
and often not for the better. I hate
thinking about this stuff; I want to
do the right thing in the big picture,
besides just helping Frank...who
suddenly loves anime?!

dynamic

THE BOTTOM DROPS OUT

MATT AND I ARE SUPER EXCITED to finally skateboard with Umberto in his sweet new chair. Even Carly wants in on the action; she's used a few of my boards over the years and insists on coming along.

"I hope Umberto doesn't rush into skateboarding headfirst—no pun intended," Carly says. We're walking to pick up Matt, then meeting Umberto at UCLA for some easy runs.

"From what I've seen of Umberto in that BMX chair, rushing into skateboarding is exactly what he has in mind." I tell her if she's going to be a worrywart, maybe she should turn around and go home.

worrywart

Just as she's about to pout, Matt skateboards down the street to meet us.

"Skateboarding with Umberto is off," he tells us.

When Carly asks if Umberto's okay, Matt is flustered by her response. "I'M the one who called it off—we have an emergency." Matt looks me straight in the eyes. "YOU have an emergency."

flustered

I beg him to tell me what's going on, but he won't say anything until we get back to his house. We jump off our decks and enter the house, where Jamie, his parents, and two men in suits pace around the kitchen.

I ask Matt for the tenth time what's going on.

Jamie is the one who answers. "Somebody in the company that produces the lottery committed fraud—he rigged the winning numbers. Now the lottery commission has frozen all the winners' money."

NO, NO, NO, NO, NO, NO, NO, NO!

"What are you talking about?" I ask. "It's impossible to fix one of those drawings! The balls come out at random! They're in a MACHINE!

fraud

The woman picks them up after they pop out!"

Matt puts his arm on mine to calm me down. "Some guy varnished six of the balls so their texture was different than the others and THOSE were the ones that fell into the chute."

varnished

chute

"WHO WOULD DO THAT?"

Matt runs his hand through his messy hair. "A guy who had his cousin in Kansas City play those exact numbers to win."

I plop onto the closest chair. One of the winners WAS from Kansas City—a man who didn't do any press or interviews.

Jamie collapses in the chair beside me. "These guys were planning it for months! The FBI just did a whole sting operation and arrested them before they did it again with a different winner this time."

I take some deep breaths. "But that has nothing to do with us! You picked those winning numbers fair and square!"

suspended

"That's what I keep telling them!" Jamie says. "But the FBI suspended the rest of the payouts while they gather evidence for the trial."

Part of me is numb, part of me wants to scream, which I end up eventually doing. "THIS ISN'T FAIR!"

attorney

One of the men I don't know approaches the table and introduces himself as Jamie's attorney. "We plan on fighting this so the suspension of funds isn't permanent."

"PERMANENT?"

Jamie's dad tells me he's talking to my parents this afternoon.

Jamie pounds on the table with his fist. "I barely have any money left! I NEED those other payments—I've got a lifestyle to maintain!"

I glance at Matt; Jamie IS in over his head with this whole thing. I'll be furious—DUH!—if the state withholds our money, but it's not like my life will be OVER. I try to imagine my parents' reaction—will they freak out or just be glad I had the chance to have this experience at all? Will they tell me to fight in court with Jamie? How long will this whole ordeal take—years? And lastly—WHO VARNISHES PING-PONG BALLS?

ordeal

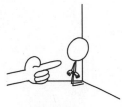

oppressive

devastated

The air in Matt's kitchen suddenly feels oppressive, so Carly and I head back to our neighborhood. I'm devastated and confused; I'm also waiting to see how long it'll be before Carly tries to find the silver lining in this DISASTER.

We haven't even reached the stop sign at the top of Matt's street when she hops off her board to face me. "Look how many great things happened with that money," she says. "Worst case—even if you never see another cent—you got some cool stuff, helped out your friends, and made a real difference in the world."

"Yeah, right," I say and smirk.

But Carly's not having it. "Just the money you gave to Greta's foundation helped demand rights for kids around the world! You empowered changemakers!"

"Well, I guess when you look at it THAT way ..."

empowered

"Not to mention the school's new media lab." She gives me a broad smile. "That IS the way to look at it. Being bummed about this whole thing would be a giant waste of time."

I kick a clump of grass growing out of the sidewalk. "Maybe I LIKE wasting time."

Carly fake-punches me in the arm. "Or maybe you can focus on something else and move on."

This time I'M the one with the broad smile. Looking at the bright side of things has always been Carly's superpower—why stop listening to her now?

We hop on our boards to tell my parents the bad news, which doesn't seem as bad anymore, thanks to Carly.

EASY COME,
EASY GO

THE NEXT FEW WEEKS ARE FILLED
with lottery commission meetings,
lawyers, and lots and lots of phone
calls. My parents handle most of it,
constantly talking with Jamie and
his parents. Wherever you go—
TV, radio, Internet—the story is
everywhere. If I begrudged Jamie
being in the spotlight when we won

begrudged

this money, I certainly wouldn't want to trade places with him now.

Carly and Umberto keep checking in with Matt and me to make sure we're okay. It's worse for me than for Matt, but he's taking Jamie's loss pretty hard too. When Saturday afternoon rolls around, the four of us are spent, just sitting in my backyard staring at the skate park.

"At least you got the first installment," Carly says in her usual positive way. "Five million dollars is an insane amount of money!"

mucky

Matt throws the mucky tennis ball up the ramp and Bodi chases after it. "Jamie and Derek could've taken the winnings up front and had ALL of the money," Matt complains. "It would take the state years to get it back—possession is nine-tenths of the law."

The phrase makes me smile and I remember back to that evening when I held the lottery ticket in my hand and they called the winning number on TV. That night I worried about whether or not to share the ticket with Jamie. Looking back now, it's like all of us have been on a roller-coaster adventure for the past few months. Do I wish things had turned out differently? YES. But do I have any right to complain? ABSOLUTELY NOT. My college tuition is paid for, I gave my friends and family great presents, I helped Frank and lots of other capuchins, the school has a new media lab, a foundation in Sweden has money to help achieve its goals, and I've got a skateboard

tuition

abruptly

park in my backyard—as well as money in the bank that the state may or may not be able to take away. The whole thing was a stroke of luck that abruptly ended, but the experience was so incredible, I wouldn't trade a minute of it.

Mom and Dad come out in their gardening clothes and immediately compliment Umberto on his new wheelchair. "Things have been so hectic, we haven't gotten a chance to see you in action," Dad says.

"I'll show you some action!" Umberto demonstrates a few freestyle spins on the grass. "You know, Derek, if you're going to ride through life's extremes, an extreme wheelchair sure comes in handy."

Umberto wheels toward the

skate park and Mom starts to worry. "Umberto, are you sure it's safe to start on the ramps?"

I'm always amazed at how much Carly and my mom have in common. Is that weird or good?

"Don't worry, Mrs. Fallon," Umberto calls from the edge of the bowl. "I've got gloves, pads, and sturdy cranial protection." He knocks on the top of his helmet twice. "All I need is someone to capture this on video."

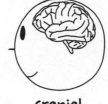

cranial

"I got you!" Dad's already framing the shot with his phone.

"Jeremy, let one of the kids film it." Mom clutches onto Dad's arm for emotional support. "Your phone should be on standby in case we need an ambulance."

ambulance

"Relax," Dad laughs and gives Mom a kiss on the cheek. "Umberto will be fine."

I'm always a little grossed out when my parents display their affection in public but seeing them be close with each other right now is actually a huge relief. Besides a ton of cash, being a millionaire brought tension into our house too. I'm glad Mom was right; our family really is stronger than that.

tension

I join Carly and Matt, who are standing a few feet behind Umberto with their own boards. I can tell from the way she's clenching her fists that Carly's as anxious as Mom is. "He took to skateboarding like a bird to the sky," I tell her. "He's been waiting for this moment for weeks."

"Hurry up already," Matt teases Umberto. "I'm not getting any younger over here!"

Umberto places his shoe on the lip of his footrest and speaks directly to Dad's camera. "Well, from my perspective, this whole thing has been one wild ride." With that, he dips down the ramp and zooms across to the other side, pausing briefly on the opposite ledge before rolling backward and hopping his chair back to the base.

"YEEEEEAAAAAAHHHHHH!!!!" I wave my board in the air like a maniac. Carly, Matt, and I surround Umberto to congratulate him on his first run in our personal skate park.

"That was INCREDIBLE!" Matt slaps Umberto on the back. "Where'd you learn to ride like that?"

"The Venice skate park," Umberto says matter-of-factly. "Duh."

Just as Matt and I are about to jump on our boards and join Umberto in the bowl, Carly elbows past us on her board and heads to the vertical ramp.

kickflip

Matt turns to me, then smiles. "Who knew Carly would have such pop on her kickflip?" Soon the four of us are careening down rails and skyrocketing off ramps with so much joy that Mr. Drake from next door comes out and stands by the fence with a cup of coffee just to take in all the fun.

careening

At one point, Bodi thinks about climbing in, but with the four of us taking turns on our runs, he retreats to the safety of the grass. I stand at the top of the bowl and take in my family, friends, dog, and neighbors: I may no longer be a billionaire with a B or a millionaire with an M, but I'm definitely lucky with a capital L.

Have you read all the books in the

My Life series?

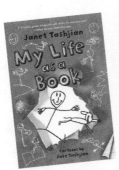

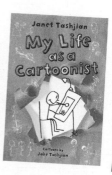

Turn the page to find out!

My Life as a Book

Derek Fallon has trouble sitting
still and reading. But creating cartoons
of his vocabulary words comes easy.
If only life were as simple!

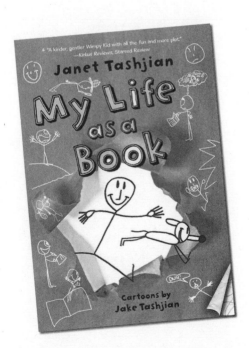

My Life as a Stuntboy

Derek Fallon gets the opportunity of a lifetime—
to be a stuntboy in a major movie—
but he soon learns that it's not as
glamorous as he thought it would be.

My Life as a Cartoonist

There's a new kid at school who
loves drawing cartoons as much
as Derek. What could be better?

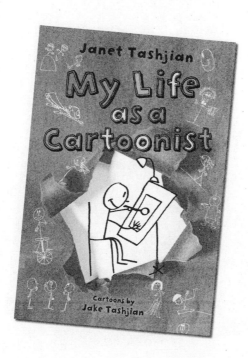

My Life as a Joke

Now in middle school, Derek just wants to feel grown-up—but his own life gets in the way, and he feels more like a baby than ever.

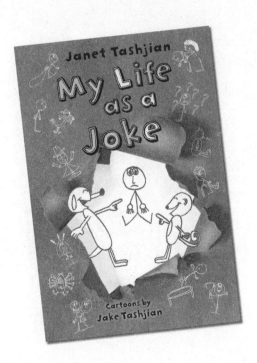

My Life as a Gamer

Derek Fallon thinks he's found his calling when he's hired to test software for a new video game. But this dream job isn't all it's cracked up to be!

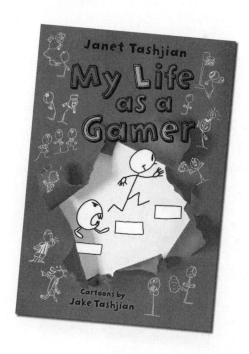

My Life as a Ninja

Derek and his friends are eager to learn more
about ninja culture. When someone starts
vandalizing their school, these ninjas-in-training
set out to crack the case!

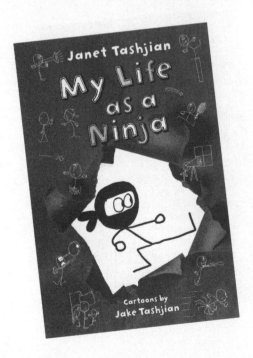

My Life as a Youtuber

Derek Fallon becomes a popular Youtuber just as his foster capuchin, Frank, must go off to monkey college, so Derek must scramble to find a reason for Frank to stay. What if Frank became a part of his Youtube videos?

My Life as a Meme

Adventures in dog-sitting for the Instagram-
famous Poufy propel Derek Fallon to more
Internet spotlight. Derek is finally a meme
legend, but it's not long before his viral
fame spins out of control!

My Life as a Coder

Derek Fallon receives an exciting new gift—a laptop! But there's a catch: It has no Wi-Fi, so he can't use it for gaming. If he wants to play computer games, he'll just have to learn how to code them himself.

About the Author

Janet Tashjian is the author of many bestselling and award-winning books, including the My Life series, the Einstein the Class Hamster series, the Marty Frye series, and the Sticker Girl series. Other books include *The Gospel According to Larry*, *Vote for Larry*, and *Larry and the Meaning of Life* as well as *Fault Line*, *For What It's Worth*, *Multiple Choice*, and *Tru Confessions*. She lives in Los Angeles, California.
janettashjian.com • mylifeasabook.com

author

About the Illustrator

Jake Tashjian is the illustrator of the My Life series and the Einstein the Class Hamster series. He has been drawing pictures of his vocabulary words on index cards since he was a kid and now has a stack taller than a house. When he's not drawing, he loves to surf, read comic books, and watch movies.
jaketashjian.com

illustrator